Super Gremlin

Lock Down Publications and Ca$h Presents

Super Gremlin

A Novel by *King Rio*

Super Gremlin

Lock Down Publications
Po Box 944
Stockbridge, Ga 30281

Visit our website @
www.lockdownpublications.com

Copyright 2023 by King Rio
Super Gremlin

Lock Down Publications
Like our page on Facebook: Lock Down Publications @
www.facebook.com/lockdownpublications.ldp
Book interior design by: **Shawn Walker**
Edited by: **Nuel Uyi**

Stay Connected with Us!

Text **LOCKDOWN** to 22828 to stay up-to-date with new releases, sneak peaks, contests and more…
Thank you.

Submission Guideline.

Submit the first three chapters of your completed manuscript to ldpsubmissions@gmail.com, subject line: Your book's title. The manuscript must be in a .doc file and sent as an attachment. Document should be in Times New Roman, double spaced and in size 12 font. Also, provide your synopsis and full contact information. If sending multiple submissions, they must each be in a separate email.

Have a story but no way to send it electronically? You can still submit to LDP/Ca$h Presents. Send in the first three chapters, written or typed, of your completed manuscript to:

LDP: Submissions Dept
Po Box 944
Stockbridge, Ga 30281

DO NOT send original manuscript. Must be a duplicate.

Provide your synopsis and a cover letter containing your full contact information.

Thanks for considering LDP and Ca$h Presents.

Dedication

I dedicate this novel in everlasting memory of Neal Wallace, Jr.

#LongLiveKingNeal

Acknowledgements

Yooo! I'm back with another gangsta book series. Y'all already know how I'm rockin'. Sit back and enjoy the read as I introduce you to a brand new collection of characters to love and hate. And shout out to Kodak Black, whose music inspired me to get back in the lab and drop some'n new. Keep steppin' on em, Yak!

Make sure y'all rock with the other amazing authors at Lockdown Publications. Shout out to Ca$h, the best urban fiction publisher in the game. To my family, I love y'all, and I can't wait to get back to Chicago to see you all. I can't forget to mention my lovely lady friend, Queen Bunny, and her exceptionally talented daughter Bean. You two funny ladies are a huge inspiration to me, as well. And to the longtime fans of my work, I worked extra hard to bring you the very best of me in this new series. I'm quite certain that neither of you will be disappointed, and if you are I'll more than make up for it in book two.

Y'all can follow me on Facebook: Author Rio

On Instagram: @authorrio5

And on Twitter: @authorrio

Undying Love, King Rio

King Rio

Prologue

April 19, 2022

Herman Patterson was a big black man with a large round beach ball of a belly. Growing up in the nineties, when the movie *Friday* became one of the most iconic hood films to ever hit the big screen, his nickname had naturally evolved from Big Herm to Big Worm. The new nickname didn't bother him at all. In fact, he loved the name so much that last summer he'd gone and purchased himself a convertible just like the real Big Worm. His was a 1964 Chevy Impala, painted candy orange and suspended high above a sparkling gold set of thirty-inch Forgiato spanked rims. He'd invested almost $120,000 in the car. It was his pride and joy and he'd even given it a name. He called it *Baby*.

He was sitting in *Baby*, parked on a dark west side street on a particularly warm mid-April night in Chicago, when his good time with a longtime side chick took a terrible turn for the worst.

Big Worm's big worm was sliding in and out of his side chick's throat, and his mind was focused on his money.

He'd had a great week, financially speaking. He had raked in $240,000 from the three kilos of heroin he'd sold over the past four days. That amount had tipped him over the five-million-dollar savings goal he'd set for himself last year on his thirty-ninth birthday. He had the cash neatly bundled in rubber bands and stuffed into eight large suitcases in a northwest Indiana storage unit.

With his savings goal reached, he was going to make tonight his very last night of windy city living. He would leave without telling a soul, move to nearby Michigan City, Indiana—where his two younger sisters and his mother lived—

and retire from the dope game for good. There were too many threats here in Chicago, too many killers and robbers lurking around every corner. Worm had been robbed three times in the past four years and shot twice. It was time to go.

Big Worm was parked in front of his Aunt Rina's house near the corner of 15th Street and Spaulding Avenue, with the top down on his Impala and his speakers blasting out the tunes of "Ahhh Ha," Lil Durk's latest drill hit. The Impala was by far the flashiest car on the street. Worm's naked ass rested comfortably on the soft leather seat beneath him as he sat taking on a Backwoods' blunt full of Black Cherry Gelato weed that had cost him six grand for a single pound. Bunny, the twenty-year-old baddie currently sliding her juicy lips up and down his dick, liked to smoke the exotic bud, so he'd brought along an ounce just for her. She had no idea that the weed was actually a going-away present. Bunny gave the best head Worm had ever gotten, and he figured what better way to end his multimillion dollar Chicago drug run than by getting the best blowjob the city had to offer.

He palmed the back of her thousand-dollar wig and pushed down. Bunny gagged as he burrowed deeper into her throat, but she didn't pull away. She *couldn't* pull away; she had a reputation to uphold. She was Yasmine "Bunny XXX" Gardan, the girl thousands of Pornhub viewers had christened the official "throat goat." Her porn videos had amassed millions of views. One video showed her sloppily sucking Worm's dick to a glorious eruption that had splattered her exceptionally pretty brown face with thick white slime.

Big Worm tilted his head back and blew a dense stream of smoke at the cloudless, star-spangled sky. He kept his hand on the back of Bunny's head as it continued to rise and fall. The head of his dick struck the rear of her throat again and again, bringing him closer to the edge with every strike.

"Don't get no nut on my seat," he said.

Bunny nodded with his length still buried in her throat. She resumed her masterful combination of bobbing and sucking. Seconds later, Big Worm tensed up and shot off into her steadily sucking mouth.

His eyes rolled up in their sockets. His breathing hitched erratically. A warm breeze soughed across the whites of his rolled-up eyes, and when the irises and pupils came back down, they glimpsed an unfamiliar face in his rearview mirror, a brown-skinned teenage boy he had never seen before. The boy was right behind the Impala, head lowered, peering in. Two car lengths behind him, a dark-colored minivan idled in the middle of the street, its headlights off, its sliding door wide open. Worm figured the boy was here for the party currently taking place in the backyard of Poochie's house across the street. It was her brother Pee Wee's thirty-fourth birthday, and they had invited half the neighborhood. The half they had invited consisted almost entirely of Traveling Vice Lords. That explained why the vigilant young gangsters who usually kept watch over higher ranking gang members like Worm were missing in action.

An arrogant smile spread across Big Worm's charcoal black face. He had just filled this young bad bitch's mouth with cum—she was still stroking and squeezing the last salty drops out of him—and here was this young broke nigga looking in from the outside, wishing he could be like Worm.

Life could not possibly get any sweeter.

Big Worm reached down to pick up his Amiri jeans.

"Wait," Bunny said, her tongue drowning in a pool of semen. She produced an iPhone from her Chanel bag and recorded video of his saliva-coated penis, then switched to the front-facing camera and opened her pretty mouth to show the fresh goo that stretched from her tongue to the roof of her mouth like rubber bands on braces. He knew she was likely recording content for her OnlyFans account. She'd made over a half million dollars uploading X-rated pics and videos to the popular site.

The boy came around to Big Worm's door just as Worm was fastening his Louis Vuitton belt. Worm took a long pull on the blunt and inhaled.

"I see you, OG," the boy said, grinning and nodding his dreadlocked head. He wore a tattered gray Nike hoodie; the hood pushed halfway back on his head, revealing an acne-scarred face. He looked past Worm. "*Damn*, who is *shorty*?"

Bunny stuck her head out over her door and spat the mouthful of semen onto the street. She turned back to the boy with a seductive smirk on her pretty brown face.

"I'm Bunny," she said. "Check me out on Only Fans. Just look for Bunny XXX. That's three X's. On TikTok my username is—"

She shut up very suddenly, her sexy expression shifting to one of alarm. Big Worm was looking at her when it happened. Her eyes got big. Her mouth fell open. She moved toward her door in a quick, shaky motion that looked like a flinch.

Something about the teen standing at Worm's door had scared all the sexy out of Bunny XXX.

Swiveling his head back toward the boy, his heart sinking to the pit of his vastly sloping stomach, Big Worm saw that the boy had drawn a black handgun and was gripping it tightly in his ashy-knuckled fist. He had the gun aimed at Big Worm's head.

In the split second before the brilliant flashes and deafening bangs began, Big Worm ducked and moved as best as his oversized body allowed. Ultimately, it did him no good. The bullets found their mark one after the other, and soon Big

Worm's heavy body was slumped forward against the steering wheel, bleeding from numerous bullet wounds.

The last thought that crossed his mind before he lost consciousness was an image: the tattoo he'd glimpsed on the front of the boy's neck, a five-pointed star with a jagged crack running down the middle, splitting it in two. It was a sign of disrespect to the Vice Lords, and 15th and Spaulding was undisputed Vice Lord territory.

It was no wonder Worm hadn't recognized the youngster. The boy was an opp from enemy territory, here to catch a TVL lacking, and Worm just happened to be outside, in the wrong place at the wrong time.

King Rio

Chapter One

July 6, 2022

"This shit better be worth a thousand damn dollars," Markio Earl muttered irritably as he raised the wide steel sliding door and stared off into the dark storage unit.

"Well, it has some nice furniture. That's what we came here to get," his girlfriend Whitney said, planting her hands on her curvaceous hips and looking around the big square room.

She was right. Markio's need for affordable furniture had been the sole purpose of their trip to the storage auction in the first place. He'd outbid four old white men and a married Hispanic couple for this particular unit after seeing the sofa and loveseat piled atop one another against the west wall. A few large mattresses and a new-looking five-piece redwood bedroom set were stored near the back wall. Eight stainless-steel suitcases and numerous transparent trash bags filled with clothes were gathered along the east wall.

Markio went to the light switch and flicked it upwards. The ceiling lights came on. He walked over to the couches and ran his fingertips along the smooth brown leather side of the sofa.

"This is brand-fucking-new, baby," he said in fluctuating tones of amazement.

Whitney followed his path to the west wall, and after her own examination of the furniture she came to the same conclusion. "It's definitely new. Shit, that's real leather too. Smell it." She leaned in and sniffed. "All this is worth way more than the thousand dollars you paid for it. Whoever defaulted on the payments for this storage locker is either dead or dead stupid."

They crossed the concrete floor to the bedroom set and spent a long silent moment admiring the luxurious wood of the dresser and bed frame. The headboard was large and padded on the front with soft tan leather. The bedside tables had two drawers each, and there were three seventy-inch televisions, still new in the boxes they came in, behind the mattresses.

Markio turned to Whitney and smiled contentedly. He eyed the profile of her sexy face, and the copious amount of ass and thighs her skin-tight Dior yoga shorts were stretched around. Every time Markio looked at his high-yellow better half, he couldn't stop himself from smiling. *How could a woman so thick and so pretty have chosen me?* he thought. Whitney Clarrett was a stunner, five foot seven with long dark hair and the kind of body a lot of women paid thousands of dollars to get. She had a large and perfectly spherical ass, and her abdomen was gym-hardened with a two-carat diamond stud pierced into her navel.

In contrast, Markio was so short as Kevin Hart—the same height, in fact—and muscular from all the weightlifting he'd done during his fifteen-year stint in the Indiana prison system. He was light-skinned and wore his hair in 360-degree waves that required daily brushing and weekly visits to Chris Diggs, his barber. He had two teardrops tatted below his left eye, and numerous other tattoos, including a huge one across the top of his back that spelled out: ALMIGHTY. He liked to consider himself a retired gang member, focused solely on Whitney and the life they were building together, but deep down he knew that the gangster spirit he'd always possessed was alive and well inside of him, festering and percolating in the darkest part of his heart, impatiently awaiting the perfect opportunity to wreak havoc yet again. Markio felt that it was likely his gangster reputation that had drawn Whitney to him from the start.

Or maybe it was his hustle. Markio had gotten out of prison early last year with more than a hundred thousand dollars in the bank, money he'd made trafficking Suboxone strips and Tunec—synthetic marijuana—into the prison through crooked guards to sell to his fellow inmates over the years. He'd bought himself an SUV—a used 2019 Mercedes-Benz GLC 300—and a new wardrobe that consisted mostly of Nike sneakers and designer jeans, shirts and hoodies. He'd used his last ten grand to buy two hundred grams of heroin, cut the grams with Dorman to double the grams, and sold each gram to local heroin addicts for $150 apiece. He'd used the proceeds to cop twenty pounds of exotic California bud, switching hustles before the feds could get on to him for dealing heroin. Exotic weed money was slower than heroin money, but Markio had no complaints. After living in a tiny one-bedroom apartment for the past year, he was finally moving into his own house, a two-story red brick home with three bedrooms, two bathrooms, and a full basement he couldn't wait to furnish. The greatest thing about the house was that it was only a block north of Whitney's place.

Whitney headed over to the plastic trash bags, jarring Markio from his thoughts. He trailed behind her, his unwavering gaze fixed on her wonderfully jiggling ass, loving the way it undulated in the tight shorts. Markio wore a black-and-gray Palm Angels jogger and white Air Force Ones of the same color. His jewelry consisted of a diamond pinky ring he'd paid almost four grand for and a rose gold Rolex wrist watch Whitney had given him for his thirty-fifth birthday back in February. Although there was nothing on his neck, he planned on buying himself a decent Cuban-link choker once he really got his money up.

Tearing a hole into the side of one bag, Whitney wrestled out the largest sweatshirt Markio had ever seen. It was a blue handed sweater with *Givenchy Paris* printed across the chest in white lettering.

"Shit, Kin, you'll get that thousand dollars back times two off this sweater alone. This is brand new too." She sniffed at the fabric and gave an approving nod, her eyes widening in surprise. "I bet this costs at least three racks. Especially in this size."

Markio stepped around her and pulled two more items from the bag: a huge black sweater with BALENCIAGA printed all over it in blue lettering, and an equally large white-and-gold Versace T-shirt. They were so new that the price tags were still attached. The price for the sweater was $3,750.00. The T-shirt's price was $1,209.00.

"Aw, *hell* yeah." Markio's face lit up. He stuffed the clothes back inside the bag. "We hit the jackpot. Let's load this shit up and ride out."

Whitney went out to the U-Haul truck and backed into the doorway of the storage unit. As she and Markio worked together carrying and positioning everything into the trailer. They had a surprisingly difficult time lifting the heavy suitcase; neither of them had a clue as to how big a jackpot they actually had in their possession.

Nor did they know of the hell that would soon be unleashed because of it.

Chapter Two

"You're awake! Yay!" Bunny cheered as she entered Worm's hospital room holding the strings of a dozen get- well-soon balloons in one hand and her iPhone in the other.

The only parts of Worm's body that moved toward the annoyingly cheerful voice were his eyes. The rest of his body was almost impossible to move without sending dull waves of pain sweeping through him.

He had been shot seven times: once through the neck, twice in the left shoulder, twice through his left forearm, once through his left wrist, and a seventh bullet had blasted off the top part of the thumb on his left hand. One of the rounds had torn through a lung, deflating the organ. Another had pierced his kidney. He'd been put in a medically-induced coma the night of the shooting, and had undergone five life-saving surgeries to repair the damage. He had awakened from the coma yesterday morning to find his two younger sisters, Star and Mya, at his bedside. Latazia and Ebony, the mothers of his two youngest sons, had popped in to check on him, and about twenty members of the Patterson family, as well as several fellow gang members, had visited with him all throughout the day. Bunny was today's first visitor, and Worm was glad to see her.

"So," she asked, "how are you feeling? Are you able to talk?"

"A little. Fuck." Worm's throat felt like sandpaper. His voice was low and hoarse, hardly even a whisper. "Shit hurts."

"I got hit too. A deep-ass graze wound across the back of my neck and another one across the bottom of my chin. I couldn't post new content for a month." Bunny approached the foot of his bed, smiling brightly and looking good enough to eat in a tight-fitting pink Fendi mini-dress over black peep-toe heels. The Birkin bag hanging down from her shoulder was a pink croc skin. "I know, I know," she said, shaking her head and raising her eyes to the ceiling. "I was only grazed twice and you got it a heck of a lot worse. I've been telling people that for weeks and weeks. I tell everybody to forget about me and to just pray for you."

"Listen. I got a few suitcases—"

"In storage?" Bunny said, finishing the sentence for him.

Big Worm gawked at her, his brow wrinkled in disbelief. He had never told *anyone* about the storage unit.

Reading his expression, Bunny smiled and said, "You're wondering how I know that, huh?" She giggled sweetly. "Some white man started blowing up your phone about a month ago. He claimed you owed money for a storage unit somewhere in Indiana. Your auntie told me about it when I stopped by there last night. She thought the old man was a scammer. To be honest, I was thinking the same thing."

Worm attempted to sit up in bed and a sharp bolt of pain thundered through his ample gut. The pain meds in his system allowed him to withstand the ache, but it still hurt. His nostrils flared against the ache. He balled his meaty right hand into a tight fist and breathed, watching Bunny's mouth fall open as the pieces came together in her mind.

"Oh shit. Shit, shit, shit," she said, enunciating each word. "There was something you really needed in there. Something important."

"Did Rina pay the man?"

"No. She blocked him after he called yesterday. She said he told her yesterday was the deadline for somebody to pay what you owe before your locker got put up for auction."

Shaking his head, Worm felt hot bile rise into his esophagus. It made his eyes water. He swallowed and took a moment to calm himself. Why had Aunt Rina answered his phone in the first place? She had money, so why hadn't she just paid the storage bill herself? Why hadn't his brother Bam paid the bill? The more questions swirled through his head, the angrier he became.

"Look," he said, "I need you to drive to Michigan City right the fuck now. Go to *Michiana Storage Masters*. Just *Google* the address. If you can get there in time, pay the bill. I got twenty racks for you if you can do that."

Bunny's thumbs were already busy typing away on her iPhone. "I'll just call now and see if they've auctioned it off yet."

It took her less than thirty seconds to *Google* the business and get someone on the line, thirty seconds that to Worm felt like thirty agonizing minutes.

On the television, CNN was showing someone's prediction of an imminent recession. Russia was still pounding Ukraine with missile strikes, which along with coronavirus, related production and shipping delays had led to skyrocketing inflation. Bitcoin was making a comeback after plummeting to under $20,000. Gas prices were on the rise, with the national average topping $5 per gallon.

None of the news interested Worm. He didn't care if Russia nuked Ukraine and gas prices rose to $100 per gallon. The only thing Worm cared about was the drug money he'd stashed away in that storage unit.

He listened anxiously to Bunny's side of the conversation: "Hello, this is Yasmine Garden, calling about a storage locker my friend rented from you all a few months back."

"I rented it a year ago," Worm corrected. "Put it on speaker."

Bunny put the call on speaker and stood next to the bed, chewing gum and smelling like heaven on earth. Normally,

Worm would have had a hard time keeping his eyes off her fat round ass, but right now her notable curves meant nothing.

"This is Herman Patterson. I actually rented the unit from you all about a year ago."

"Hello, Mr. Patterson. I'm Melissa Starks with Michiana Storage Masters. How may I help you?"

"I rented a storage locker in August of last year. I was shot and seriously injured a few months ago, and I was put into a medically induced coma until yesterday morning. I've just learned that I have received several calls from your business regarding my outstanding storage fees."

"Ohhh. I know who you are. My boss has been trying to reach out to you. Hold on. I'll go and find him."

She put him on hold. Worm shut his eyes and tilted his head back. He inhaled deeply and exhaled slowly and grimaced at the subtle sting in his healing lung. *Please, God, please let my money be there,* he prayed. *I'll never in my life sell another gram of dope. Just let my money be there.*

Bunny began pacing a tight circle beside Worm's bed, nibbling at the corner of her bottom lip, her designer heels tapping melodically on the tiled linoleum floor. Worm could see the graze wound on the nape of her neck, but only because he was looking for it. The scar had healed over well.

"Fuck my life," she said in a low, thoughtful tone. "I should have just paid the bill myself. I should've offered to pay for it. But I honestly believed it was a scam. Like the time that man called your sister after your pops died saying your daddy had an account with Chase Bank that had her listed as the sole beneficiary, and all he needed was your dad's social security number and date of birth to send her the check."

Worm remembered that one well. The guy had created an online banking account in his later father's name, opened a line of credit, and used it to order thousands of dollars' worth of jewelry and electronic appliances. Worm hadn't known the full gist of the scam until the IRS contacted his mother months later. Jesse Mae Lee, formerly Jesse Mae Patterson, had been married to Leroy Henry Patterson for forty-one years. They had divorced in 2015, a year before Leroy was shot and killed in the crossfire of a gang-related shooting while driving home from a doctor's appointment. Like Leroy Patterson's shooter, the scammer had never been identified.

Melissa Starks came back on the line. "I'm sorry, Mr. Patterson. My boss is busy right now. He's helping out with the auctions. I'll have him give you a call as soon as he's free."

As Bunny ended the call, Worm clenched his teeth and seethed. After a long silent moment of rumination, he turned to Bunny. She was all ears, arms folded over her buxom chest, legs scissored, eyes focused on his.

"They're doing the auction right now," he said finally. "The storage locker number is C-15. I'll give you fifty thousand dollars if you can get there in time to get that locker. And if you can't get there in time, find out who bought it." He paused, thinking, then added: "*I need that locker.* Do you understand me? Do *whatever* you have to do to get it. No pit stops. Go."

Bunny nodded vehemently. She gave Worm a quick kiss on the cheek and then left the room in a hurry.

Worm muted the television, took another deep breath, and shut his eyes for second prayer, hoping with every drop of hope in his soul that God would intervene on his behalf.

If the good Lord didn't take the wheel, Worm's older brother—Bam—had an army of Vice Lords in the north Lawndale neighborhood, the hood where Bam and Worm had grown into men, the trenches where Worm was shot and nearly killed almost three months ago. An order from Bam was never ignored. Worm hoped it wouldn't come to that, but he needed these eight suitcases back in his possession, and he was willing to do whatever it took to make that happen.

Chapter Three

"Ugh, I am so tired of this thirsty-ass nigga," Whitney complained, staring at her buzzing iPhone and ignoring the incoming call.

It was a call from Black Jimmy, deadbeat father to Whitney's seventeen-year-old son James "Lil' Jimmy" Thomas, Jr. Whatever Black Jimmy was calling for, Whitney was not trying to hear it. She turned her attention back to the shirtless figures of Markio and his friend—Fat Jerm. She was watching them as they carried the sofa up the front porch steps and in through the open front door of Markio's new home.

She was sitting in Markio's air-conditioned SUV. As always, she was beyond happy to be behind the wheel of the sparkling white Mercedes, with the butter-soft leather seat beneath her and all the high-tech gadgetry at her fingertips. Her own vehicle was a 2021 Honda Accord, nice but nowhere near as gaudy as the Benz.

Her iPhone stopped ringing, but only momentarily. Within seconds, Black Jimmy was calling again, blowing her up like he always did when she ignored him. She looked back out the window and laughed once as she watched Fat Jerm's younger brother—Josh—struggle carrying one of the televisions up the steps. When her phone rang again, it was a FaceTime call from her younger sister, Candace, and she answered immediately.

"Where you at?" This was Candace's opening line to every phone call she made. Caramel brown and just as stunning as her big sister, Candace was Whitney's best friend and closest confidant. Her hair was colored blue and styled in a neat shoulder-length bob. Beads of sweat glistened on her face.

"I'm around the corner from the house. Why, what's up?"

"Where at, around the corner?"

"On Vail Street. At Markio's house. I told you he got the house Destiny used to stay in. Oouu, and it's nice in there too." Whitney paused to take a long swallow from her cold bottle of Aquafina water. "He just got some good ass furniture from the storage auction. I told you we should've gone to that last one. Markio got a brand-new leather sofa with a matching love seat, a brand new five-piece bedroom set, three seventy-inch TVs, and like ten bags full of designer clothes. And he only paid a thousand dollars for all of it."

Candace's eyebrows shot up.

"I know, right?" Whitney's brow rose too. "And he got some big steel suitcases with locks on 'em. I don't know what's in them, but they are heavy as fuck."

Candace smirked. "You love that man."

Whitney nodded smilingly "I do, sis. I can't even cap, I am really, truly in love with that lil' nigga. He's the only man I've ever had who actually gets me. And he ain't for every-body. He's the most loyal man I've ever been with. He's a hustler. He's respected in the streets. He takes good care of me, and my kids love him. It's like I'm in a dream."

Candace was nodding understandingly. Whitney spotted the "Employees Only" sign on the wall behind Candace and knew that her sister was in the break room at Olive Garden, where she worked as a server.

"Did Black Jimmy call you?" Candace asked.

"Mmhm. Like four times in a row."

"Don't answer. He just called me asking where to find you. He said it was important, but he sounded drunk or high on somthin'."

Black Jimmy had a habit of calling Whitney when he was tipsy, sometimes to argue but usually because the drugs and alcohol made his dick hard and he needed a hot wet pussy to stick it in. Whitney had fallen for it hundreds of times in the past, but she wouldn't do it again. She was over him. Markio had her heart. And besides, Markio's sex game was way better than Jimmy's.

"Let me get back out here," Candace said, toweling the sweat from her face and glancing at someone off screen. "I'll call you when I get off."

After the video call with Candace, Whitney went to a group chat she had with her kids—17-year-old Lil' Jimmy, 16-year-old twins: Ava and Eva; and 14-year-old Joselyn— and sent them a message: "Ava, I need you to pick up four large pizzas, three orders of hot wings, some cheese sticks, and a two-liter of Pepsi from Pizza Hut. That's dinner 'cause I'm not cooking. And my gas tank better not be on E. I want y'all home by eight."

Thinking of the twins made Whitney think of their father, Jarvell "Veezo" Holmes, who'd been dead going on three years now. She'd gotten back with him when they took the kids to Disneyland to celebrate Eva and Ava's thirteenth birthday. Whitney had tried to make it work. The thing was, she'd already had an ongoing fling with one of Veezo's closest friends when she and Veezo got back together, and she had been too selfish to put an end to the fling. All had gone well until just three months after the Disneyland trip. Veezo returned home from work earlier than usual and found Whitney sitting naked on the edge of their bed, her legs spread wide and drawn back while his close friend kneeled on the floor in front of her, fingering her pussy and rapidly drumming the flat of his tongue against her engorged clitoris. Veezo had attempted to strangle Whitney right there on the spot, clamping his strong black hands around her neck and squeezing with all his might. She was seeing spots of black and on the verge of losing consciousness when she snatched the Ruger handgun from his waist and shot him through the ribcage, just under his left pectoral muscle. As he stumbled back, clutching at the bullet wound, Whitney had raised the gun and shot him twice more in the chest. He'd died within minutes.

Veezo's friend later gave a statement to police alleging that Veezo had walked into the bedroom and attacked Whitney without provocation. She had taken the insurance company to court over the policy she'd put on him years prior, and in the end the dispute was settled and she received the full $175,000 insurance payment, which she used to buy her house and start her cosmetics business.

Whitney looked out the window at Markio and Fat Jerm. They were standing side by side on the porch, sweating and laughing about something. Whitney took a moment to admire Markio's sharply defined six-pack. One of the many things she loved to do to Markio was kissing her way down his chest, taking her time to lick and suck on each individual brick of abdominal muscle.

Her gaze drifted over to Fat Jerm. He was light brown in complexion like Markio, just under six feet tall and maybe two hundred forty pounds. His teeth were gold and he was wearing a diamond necklace with an icy "10th Street" pendant that had to have cost him ten or fifteen grand. Sweat trickled down from his bald head to his flabby man boobs and sluiced down over his wide, six-packless belly, dampening the waistline of his fitted purple jeans.

Looking at Jerm, Whitney wondered whether he'd ever told anyone the true story about the night Veezo came home and caught him with his pants down to his knees and his face between her thighs. She wondered if he'd revealed to Markio that they had been sneaking and linking for a good five months back in 2019, and that every now and then they still *FaceTime* each other to reminisce.

Super Gremlin

She hoped to God he'd kept his mouth shut, but she couldn't be sure.

King Rio

Chapter Four

Bunny had traveled to Indiana twice in the past three years, the first time being when her then boyfriend, Quentin, a 6'7" professional bodyguard twenty years her senior, had taken her to a Chris Brown concert at the Lucas Oil Stadium in Indianapolis. She was only seventeen at the time, but Quentin had somehow managed to get her a backstage pass, and she'd been able to meet her lifelong celebrity crush in the hallway outside of his dressing room, even managing to give him a hug and a fast kiss on the cheek before Quentin dragged her away.

Her second visit to the Hoosier State had taken place late last summer, to shoot a porn scene for Lucid Entertainment at a beachfront mansion in Michigan City. The payday was only $3,500, but the publicity she gained from working with one of the adult film industry's leading studios had changed the trajectory of her career in a very big way. Since then, Bunny XXX's bookings had shot through the roof, with everything from hosting parties that paid $25,000 or better to being an announcer and first-time nominee at the upcoming AVN Awards. And there was one thing Bunny had to admit: without Big Worm's financial backing, none of her newfound fame would have been possible.

Worm had paid for the breast enhancement and fat transfer surgeries Bunny underwent two months before the filming of her first official porn scene, taking out what she'd called the "pooch" in her stomach and the unsightly folds on her sides, narrowing her waist and thickening her ass. He'd dropped over twenty thousand dollars on her veneers, giving her the flawless smile she'd always wanted, and he'd even slipped her landlord $60,000 in cash so she could live rent-free in her million-dollar Streeterville condo for an entire year. If not for

Worm's generosity, Bunny knew that her lifestyle would be nowhere near as easy to maintain as it was now.

So when she arrived at Michiana Storage Masters in her cherry-red Range Rover, vibing along to the beat as a Glo-Rilla song boomed from her speakers, Bunny's mind was set on doing exactly as Worm had asked, no matter the trouble or difficulty.

She parked and walked thirty feet through blistering July heat to the storage business's small office building. With beads of perspiration already sprouting from her pores, she pulled open the cheap, cream-colored wooden door and stepped inside.

A cool, stale breeze blew at her face. The air-conditioning units were running loud and hard, pushing around the horrid stench of the place. A pale, white woman with curly red hair and freckles sat behind a weathered faux wood desk. Bunny looked at the nametag pinned to the woman's shirt: *M. Starks*.

"Excuse me," Bunny said in her sweetest tone of voice. "I believe we spoke on the phone about an hour ago. I'm Yasmine Gordon, and I'm here about Mr. Herman Patterson's storage locker."

Melissa looked up at Bunny, a pair of tortoise-framed eyeglasses resting on the very tip of her nose, her forehead wrinkled with age. The woman was older than she'd sounded on the phone. She was in her mid-forties at the very least, her red hair sprinkled with strands of gray, crow's feet at the corners of her Mediterranean brown eyes.

"I'm sorry to inform you, but the auction is over," Melissa Starks said. "The time for Mr. Patterson to pay his outstanding storage fee is long past due. His locker was sold off to the highest bidder toward the very beginning of the auction."

"To whom?"

"I'm not at liberty to disclose that information."

Bunny exhaled nasally, rolled her eyes, and squinted at the corpse-pale lady. "Listen, I am willing to pay you five thousand dollars in crispy new hundreds for the name of the person who bought that locker." She dug in her purse and pinched out a ten-thousand-dollar packet of hundreds. "The ashes of Herman Patterson's late father were in that storage locker. All I need is a name, and fifty of these Benjamins are yours."

Melissa sat back in her creaky old office chair. She crossed her arms and studied Bunny for a couple of seconds. She leaned to the side and looked past Bunny, peering out the dirt-spotted front windows. Then she moved forward and whispered, "I'd give you my left tit for five grand. Wait one second. I just filed the bill of sale."

She spun around and stood and went to the row of filing cabinets that lined the wall behind her swivel chair, while Bunny tore the gold and white paper wrap off the packet of hundreds and counted out fifty of them. Melissa turned back to Bunny and placed the single sheet of paper in front of her, painting a pearly polished green fingernail at a name and address: Whitney L. Clarrett, 302 E. Comb Street. There was also a phone number. Bunny used her smartphone to snap a few pics of the document. Then she handed over the cash and left the office building in a hurry, dialing the number to Worm's hospital room as she sped-walked back to her Range Rover.

The line was still ringing when she settled into the driver's seat, as she ended the call and phoned Worm's brother—Bam.

King Rio

Chapter Five

Bam would not receive the call.

Minutes before Bunny's call, Bam had turned on his smartphone's *Do Not Disturb* feature and shut off every alert.

His blacked-out Dodge Challenger Hellcat was parked near the northeast corner of Erie and Lavergne, in a west side Chicago neighborhood he rarely ever visited. He was parked just two houses down from his target's home address, which the target's ex-girlfriend had confirmed was 4954 W. Erie Street. The target's name was Eric Shaw, according to the disgruntled ex who'd collected the ten grand Bam had offered for the location and identity of Big Worm's shooter. The name Eric used as an up-and-coming drill rapper was Wack-a-Man. He was a member of the Simon City Royals, a street gang that had long ago declared war against numerous sets of Traveling Vice Lords.

The stone-faced young man seated next to Bam was also an aspiring rap artist, albeit a poorly skilled one. He went by the name Baby Lord, and his true talent was his impressive speed and remarkable aim. He had dark skin and short hair styled into waves. The lower half of his face was hidden behind a COVID-19 mask, and the rest of his head was wedged inside the tightly drawn head of his black Chrome Hearts hoodie. Baby Lord's left hand was clamped tight around the handle of a Glock 23 pistol with an attached 50-round drum magazine and a custom switch that allowed the gun to fire on fully automatic.

"Get up close and knock his head off his shoulders," Bam said, his diamond teeth twinkling brilliantly in the sunlight as he eyed his own reflection in the rearview mirror. "I don't want his mama to recognize him by nothin' but the clothes on his back."

Baby Lord nodded and said nothing.

Like his younger brother Worm, Bam was a big-time heroin dealer. He was tall, dark, and bald, and there was never a moment when he didn't fit the typical drug-dealer stereotype. He only wore the latest in designer fashion, and every piece of jewelry he owned was flooded with flawless white diamonds, everything from his Cuban-link necklaces and bracelets to his high-end wrist-watches. Twenty of his teeth were covered in VVS diamonds, courtesy of celebrity jeweler Johnny Dang. Bam was the most lit forty-one-year-old dope boy in the Windy City, and just about everyone knew it. The twelve city blocks his gang had complete control over made him around $100,000 per day. He also sold large quantities of heroin and fentanyl to other Chicago dealers.

Bam had a reputation for being one of the most ruthless gang leaders in the city, known for placing bounties that often exceeded $50,000 on the heads of his opposition. Which was nothing compared to the seven million dollars he had put away in a spare room at his South Florida summer home, or the $1.8 million in cash he had locked away in the shed behind his mother's three-acre property in Michigan City, Indiana.

So the $100,000 he was paying Baby Lord for Eric Shaw's murder was chump change.

There was a second blacked-out Hellcat parked at the opposite end of the street. Baby Lord's cousin—Ace—was waiting inside it, his long dreads hanging down over his face. His miniature Draco assault rifle held a 70-round drum.

Two minutes later, the wrought-iron gate at 4954 W. Erie Street swung open, and out stepped Eric Shaw. He had cut off his dreads, but the photograph Eric's ex had shown to Bam and the young man Bam was looking at now were definitely the same person.

Super Gremlin

Baby Lord threw open his door and ran down the sidewalk toward Eric, moving faster than Bam had ever seen a man run. Baby Lord was six feet tall and lean as can be, and he ran like an Olympic gold medalist. His cousin was no slowpoke either, crossing the street with lightning speed and making a Lexus SUV screech to a stop to avoid hitting him.

Eric saw them coming almost immediately but there was nothing he could do to stop the inevitable. His eyes widened at the sight of Ace running straight at him. He pivoted and tried to run, but he hadn't made it a single step when Baby Lord raised the Glock and sent a rapid burst of eight blue-tipped 40-caliber rounds through Eric's upper back with a single half-second squeeze of the trigger. He was going down, falling forward into the spray of blood that had just exploded from his chest, when Ace raised the Draco and fired off three quick shots. One round missed its mark, and the other two hit Eric high in the right shoulder and spun him halfway around just before he hit the ground.

He landed on his back with his legs crossed at the ankles and his arms outstretched on either side of him. Blood bubbled up out of his mouth and spilled down the sides of his acne-scarred face, and he kept opening and closing his hands and blinking his wide, frightened eyes as Baby Lord and Ace ran up and stood over him.

The two cousins aimed at Eric's face and sent over sixty shots through his skull, leaving a spattered mass of blood, bone, and brain matter splashed across the cracked slab of the sidewalk.

King Rio

Chapter Six

It had taken Markio and Whitney almost ninety minutes to put together the king-size bed frame and get the dresser and bedside tables positioned to their liking. Another half hour was lost hanging up the television. Afterwards, sticky with sweat and exhausted from all the heavy moving and lifting, Markio showered in his new bathroom while Whitney spruced up his bedroom a bit, spraying Windex on the dresser mirror and wiping it down, putting away his clothes in the dresser drawers, and sweeping his bedroom floor for the third time since he'd received the house keys from his landlord.

The first thing Markio did when he rented the U-Haul was transport all of his things from his old one-bedroom tenement at Southgate Apartments here to the house on Vail Street. With the assistance of Fat Jerm and Josh, he'd carried the old living room furniture down to the basement to make room for the new furniture he'd gotten at the storage auction, leaving only his wooden coffee table and dining table on the first floor. Curtains and Venetian blinds were hung over all the windows. The refrigerator and kitchen cabinets were densely stacked with food and beverages. His sweatshirts and jackets and heavy winter coats were on hangers in his bedroom closet, his expensive sneaker collection stacked in boxes on the floor beneath them.

This new place was already starting to feel like a home.

After the shower, he left the bathroom in his boxer-briefs and joined Whitney in the bedroom. She was on her knees on the floor, going through the clothes from the trash bag they'd gotten from the storage auction. He saw that she had put fresh linen on the bed, linen she'd found in one of the trash bags, brand-new two-tone brown Louis Vuitton sheets and a matching fur blanket.

"That's an eighty-five-hundred-dollar blanket," Whitney said excitedly. "I just *Googled* it. The sheets cost twenty-five hundred. I'm telling you, whoever owned this stuff was rich."

Markio smiled toothily at the great news, nodding. He threw on a gray pair of purple jeans and gray-and-white Nike Vapor Max sneakers, then leaned back against the redwood dresser and brushed his hair while scrolling through his new text messages.

His mom, Jeanette, needed cigarettes; his sister, Taquisha, needed to "borrow" a hundred dollars, money he knew from experience would never be repaid; his ex, Tasha, was apparently missing him, despite her being pregnant with twins by her current boyfriend; and Mya, a badass redbone he'd met at a gas station two days ago, wanted to buy another ounce of gelato. He replied to all of them: thumbs up emojis to mama and Taquisha, a side-eye emoji to Tasha, and to Mya he wrote, "30 minutes."

He set the phone face down on the dresser and crossed his strong brown arms over his bare chest. His gaze wavered from an oversized pair of Amiri jeans Whitney was folding to the eight suitcases standing a few feet away from his open closet door.

They stood back to back, in two rows of four. Stainless steel with combination locks keeping them shut. Adjustable black rubber handles sticking up from their backs. There were wheels under each suitcase.

"You try opening one of those, yet?" Markio asked without looking at Whitney.

"Yeah. They're all locked. You'll have to break them open."

Markio nodded again, staring vacantly at the suitcases, their contents as mysterious as the identity of their previous owner.

After a moment, Markio's mind wandered elsewhere.

He thought of Mya, the impossibly attractive redbone he'd first seen at the BP gas station near his former apartment two days prior, while she was pumping gas into her matte black Mercedes G-Wagon. His first view of her was a mouth-watering back shot as he had cruised onto the platform. She'd worn a white Gucci ensemble of a bucket hat, a crop-top, and booty shorts, her thick ass protruding out of the tight shorts like an overripe pumpkin. Her small and delicate feet showed through transparent t-strap wedges, the white-tipped toenails complementing her matching fingernails. Markio had parked his compact Mercedes SUV at the pump directly ahead of her full-size one and waved to her as he inserted his gas card into the machine.

"Hey, beautiful," he'd shouted.

She'd waved back and smiled at him with luscious pink glossed lips and perfect white teeth. The rest of her pie-shaped visage was just as flawless, from the blood-colored mane of hair that fell down like a short, smoothly flowing waterfall around her neck to her light brown eyes and diamond-studded left nostril.

"Hey! Good morning," she'd replied, eyeing the saucy Alexander McQueen outfit he wore before shifting her bright-eyed gaze to his compact SUV. "Okay! Let me find out we done started a Benz truck club out here." Then an incredibly sexy laugh had burst from her, high-pitched and gentle, filling Markio's soul with a lust for more.

He'd told her his name, told her he sold two-hundred-dollar quarter ounces of gelato, and she'd reached into the G-Wagon and fished two $100 bills out of a large Gucci shoulder bag. She'd bought two more quarter ounces from him yesterday, having him meet her at the Dairy Queen on Michigan Boulevard for the first transaction and back at the BP for the second. If not for his relationship with Whitney, Markio knew he would have been going above and beyond to win over the short and incredibly sexy young woman. But as it stood, he already had a bad bitch, and he planned to build an empire with her before he popped the big question, so that one day he could have her flexing in a G-Wagon just like Mya.

Thinking of Mya in those tight little booty shorts had done something to Markio: his dick had thickened, lengthened and hardened. It created a notable bulge in the front of his jeans.

He hadn't even noticed that Whitney was still babbling about all the money he would make from reselling the designer gear she was folding and organizing in piles on the hardwood floor. He had unconsciously tuned her out, his thoughts having been completely consumed by images of Mya.

He snapped out of it when Whitney looked up at him and abruptly stopped talking.

"Ummm," she said, slowly rising from her knees and tossing aside the Balenciaga scarf she'd been in the process of folding. "You need some help with that?"

Markio grinned. He thought in that moment that Whitney bore a striking resemblance to legendary R&B songstress Keke Wyatt. There was on small black beauty spot above the lip, and Whitney was much thicker in all the right places, but everything else was undeniably similar. The shape of her face, her complexion, her distinctive smile.

She moved toward him with her eyes aimed low.

"Who do we contact to sell all this shit? You need to be *Googling* that," Markio said.

Whitney ignored him and undid his pants, yanking them and his boxer-briefs down around his knees as she squatted down before him. Taking the hard length of his dick in her hand, she stroked it and spat on it. She planted a loud, smacky kiss on the head. "I'll take care of this for you," she said, and closed her mouth around his titanium erection.

Markio bit down on his bottom lip and looked down at her, resting his hands on the dresser behind him. He loved the firm suction and the wet, warm feel of her tongue and the roof of her mouth squeezing his most sensitive muscle between them as her lips moved back and forth along his formidable length.

This was another reason why Markio was so committed to loving Whitney the right way. She knew him too well. If there was one thing he loved more than getting money, it was getting his dick sucked, and Whitney gave some of the best head he'd ever received, real porn-star quality fellatio.

He curled his toes in his Nikes and inhaled shakily while Whitney cradled his balls in one hand and stroked his dick in the other as she noisily slurped him in and out of her mouth. His eyelids fluttered, then he settled his eyes on one of the bedside tables. For a long while he stared at the items he'd left there on the table before going to the shower: a fourth-generation Glock 19 pistol with an extended 30-round magazine and green laser sighting; a thick, rubber-banded cash pile of twenties, fifties, and hundreds; a brown leather wallet, and his key ring. The pile of cash amounted to just over eight thousand dollars. He had another twenty-one grand stuffed inside a cheap black backpack on the top shelf in his closet, and he still had sixteen pounds of vacuum-sealed gelato stashed away in a large duffel bag in one of the spare bedroom closets upstairs. He'd already put a padlock on that bedroom door.

Markio loved Whitney to death, but when it came to his money, he didn't trust a soul. Not even his blood relatives. He'd learned the hard way when, just a month after his release from prison, his first-cousin Mykia and his then-girlfriend Kyla had stolen seven thousand dollars from him and used it to move away and start a new life together in Louisville, Kentucky. He'd been tempted to hunt them down and put a bullet in each of their skulls, but instead he'd used the betrayal as motivation to hustle harder.

Whitney lowered her hands to her knees and started sucking Markio's dick with just her mouth, causing his breaths to become shakier as he looked down at her again. Seconds later, he reached back and put her hair up in a ponytail, moving it out of her way so she could really get at him.

His smartphone rang on the dresser behind him. He picked it up and saw that the caller was Crasher, a Gangster Disciple from the south side of Chicago. Markio had done time with him at Branchville Correctional Facility in southern Indiana. Crasher had two baby mamas who sold weed and pills for him in St. Paul, Minnesota. He smoked a lot of his own supply of weed, but he always had his hands in on one scheme or another, and he knew how to manage his habits and run up a bag. He'd only been free for two months and had already gone live on Instagram with $100,000 in hundreds spread across the hood of a dark blue Dodge Charger SRT.

The call went unanswered. Markio decided he would call Crasher back when he was in his truck, on his way to meet up with Mya.

Mya!

Her gorgeous smiling face reappeared in his mind like a divine prophecy. When he'd met up with her at the Dairy Queen, she was sitting in her truck with a girl who was darker and taller than her but just as breathtakingly attractive. She'd introduced the girl as her sister, but she hadn't given a name. Or maybe she had; Markio couldn't remember. He'd been too busy watching Mya's searching eyes as she stared out her window at him, studying his arms and his lips and his fingers.

Super Gremlin

Now he envisioned Mya squatting before him instead of Whitney, and this pushed him over the edge. He tensed and trembled as his ejaculate spewed forth into Whitney's mouth. Usually, she would pull back and let it splash onto her face and across her outstretched tongue, looking up at him as she squeezed and pulled on his dick until every last drop was out of him; she didn't mind catching the cum, but she wasn't all that fond of swallowing it. This time, however, she pressed her head towards his convulsing abdomen, burying his dick deep in her throat and taking his cum right down her esophagus.

***

Whitney absolutely hated swallowing semen. Especially Markio's. His balls expelled huge cum shots, the kind that could blind a bitch for a week if she wasn't careful. But she swallowed all of it this time, and for a good reason: she wanted in on the money Markio would get from reselling the clothes she'd found in the trash bags, and whatever else was stuffed in those eight heavy suitcases.

She figured the resale value was somewhere around $90,000, maybe more. If he gave her just $30,000 out of that, she'd be able to increase production and marketing for iKiss, her independently owned line of cosmetics. She would also be able to afford the down payment on the new Cadillac Escalade she'd been wanting ever since she saw Regina King driving one in a Super Bowl commercial early last year.

She had some ideas for the money that could benefit Markio as well. During his many years in prison, he had penned more than twenty books, gritty urban fiction novels depicting the real-life joys, struggles, and dangers of being black in America. Markio rarely spoke of his books anymore, but he still wrote on his iPhone when he didn't have anything better to do, and on his laptop when they were in bed together and he didn't feel like watching whatever reality show she was watching. Markio could very easily take ten or twenty grand and self-publish his own novels, or type them all up and find an agent who could get him a good publishing deal. Maybe he'd even get one of his book series made into a franchise of movies. The possibilities were endless, but only if he put in the effort and invested in himself.

For these reasons, Whitney planned to keep him in sight until they sorted through the last few trash bags, as well as the eight suspiciously heavy stainless steel suitcases.

Rising to her feet, Whitney used the back of her hand to wipe the gleaming ring of saliva from around her mouth. She stared down at his dick. It was still in the throes of orgasm, twitching spasmodically with a copious amount of saliva coating its softening length.

"Damn," Markio muttered breathlessly. "You tryna get a ring, ain't you? That kinda shit right there gon' get you a ring." He chuckled aloud.

Whitney's long eyelashes flustered as she rolled her eyes. She snickered, shaking her head. "Boy, get dressed so we can go. I know you got sales to make, and I need to stop by my place before we hit the streets. I'm grabbing a change of clothes so I can shower when we get back."

She turned to leave the bedroom, but Markio slipped his muscular brown arms around her waist and pulled her back against him. He kissed the nape of her neck. Ran his hands down her hips and massaged her pussy print with his fingertips.

"Baby, on Vice Lord," he said, his breath warming the back of her ear, "that was the best head I ever had in my whole

life. You ever give that mouth to another nigga—I'm shootin'
you *and* him."

Whitney only smiled.

She had Markio right where she wanted him.

King Rio

Chapter Seven

Fifteen minutes later, Markio was parked behind a cherry-red Range Rover across the street from Whitney's house. He wore a white t-shirt with a gray horizontal rectangle across the chest that had PURPLE stenciled through it in white lettering, perfectly fitting his jeans and sneakers. His eyes were concealed behind chic Cartier sunglasses. He may not have had much in the form of savings, but one thing Markio always did was dress to impress, even when no one else was looking.

He'd received four more texts from people wanting to buy weed. He sent the same reply to everyone: "OTW." *On the way.* He had a quarter pound of gelato, a box of sandwich bags, and a digital scale tucked away in one of Whitney's old purses behind the backseat, more than enough to get him through the day.

He drummed his fingertips on the wood grain of his steering wheel, looking ahead at a Chicago Bears sticker on the darkly tinted rear window of the Range Rover, waiting on Whitney to return with her change of clothes. He looked down at the Rover's license plate and saw that it was an Illinois plate. His mouth formed an intrigued smirk, and he nodded in slight admiration. He'd never seen a red Range Rover before. Then again, having been incarcerated from age nineteen to age thirty-four, there was a lot he hadn't seen.

Markio's iPhone buzzed with another text from Mya: "I'm at 1004 W. 8th Street. How long you gon be? Bc I can come to you."

What the fuck? Markio's brow moved up high on his forehead. He could not believe it. The address to his sister Taquisha's house, where she stayed on the first floor of the two-flat with her oldest son Tyquan and her boyfriend Moe, was 1006 W. 8th Street. Their mother Jeanette lived in the second-floor apartment.

Their address was directly next door to the house where Mya wanted her weed delivered.

Thinking Mya was being funny, that she had somehow learned of his family's address and was using the neighboring address to fuck with him, he decided to *FaceTime* her.

He glanced across the street to make sure Whitney wasn't walking back to the truck as he made the video call. She wasn't, but she'd left her front door halfway open. Her fenced-in yard was mostly free of the cigarette butts, snack wrappers, beer bottles, and other detritus that blighted the yards of her Comb Street neighbors. The street was just one block long, with a railroad track at the back end and a busy boulevard at the front. Five houses on Whitney's side of the street, four houses and a florist's shop on the other. The house nearest the train track on Whitney's side of the street was a drug house. A Gangster Disciple called Pimp and his Joker Mob gang trapped out of it day and night.

Markio was watching a disturbingly thin white woman with a wad of dollars clenched tight in one bony fist walk up to the front porch of the drug house when Mya's heartachingly beautiful face appeared on his phone screen.

"Oh wow," she said, smiling. "So, we're *FaceTiming* each other now? Didn't know we were doing that, but okay."

Markio's face lit up with a beaming smile of his own. He couldn't help it. Mya was too pretty, her energy too radiant. Her sister, who was darker, appeared over her shoulder and waved.

"Where y'all at?" he asked.

"I just sent you the address," Mya said, feigning an attitude.

"I know that. Who do you *know* there?"

"Why you need to know all that?"

Markio shrugged. "Just curious."

"I don't think that's any of your business. But you know what? I *did* hear that you got family in the house next door." Mya's smile grew wider. "Nah, let me stop playing. Our friend Nissa stays here. She works with my sister at St. Anthony's Hospital. My sister just became a phlebotomist a few months ago, and Nissa's an RN."

"A phlebota-what?"

Mya laughed. "She does the blood work."

"Oh." Markio nodded, thought it over, then added, "And she be high? Working with needles?"

"Are you a detective or a weed man?"

Now Markio laughed. "I'm on my way over there now."

"Really? Because from here it looks like you're sitting still."

"I promise, I'm on the way," he reiterated.

"You better be," Mya said, and ended the call.

Markio shook his head and started texting back and forth with Crasher, who wanted to buy two pounds of gelato. He talked Markio down to nine grand for the two pounds. Markio was in too good a mood not to show a little love, and since his exotic weed plug only charged him $2,300-a-pound, he'd still profit close to seven grand.

He had just finished texting with Crasher when a text from Whitney came through. "Just go on and do whatever you need to do. I'll shower and change now. Come pick me up in about an hour or so."

Markio exhaled a huge sigh of relief. The very last thing he wanted to do was meet up with Mya while Whitney was riding along with him. He shifted into *drive* and swerved out around the Rover, the sweet sound of Mya's infectious laugh still echoing through his brain.

Had he turned to look at the Range Rover as he passed it, he'd have noticed that the girl behind the wheel was staring hard at Whitney's half-open front door.

***

"Is that Whitney Clarrett in the video you just sent me?"

"I'm guessing it is. She walked into 302 East Comb Street, and she used a key to get in. It has to be her. And look." Bunny raised her iPhone, switching to the rear camera and aiming it at the front of a two-story burgundy house. "Her front door is wide open. You need to hurry up and get somebody out here."

Big Worm winced at the slight ache in his gut as Bam hit a bump in the road. The two thirty-milligram Oxycodone pills he'd swallowed five minutes earlier were beginning to work through him, and Bam's matte black Rolls Royce practically floated down the highway, but Worm still felt the ache.

He'd had his son Lil' Worm's mom—Latazia—bring him his phone and a Palm Angels jogger that was loose enough around the middle to keep the pressure off his bandages. Then he'd checked himself out of Mt. Sinai Hospital—much to his doctor's disapproval—and had Bam pick him up. He'd told Bam everything about the money in the suitcases; it was the only way to convey the true urgency of the matter. Now they were roaring down the interstate in a $450,000 Cullinan, with two black Challenger Hellcats filled with heavily armed gang members trailing close behind them.

"Just stay there and make sure she don't leave," Worm said to Bunny. "Follow her if she leaves. We'll be there in about forty, forty-five minutes."

"Okay, but I'm about to find a restaurant and get me something to eat. I'm hungry, and all I had this morning was a bowl of cereal."

"You can wait forty-five minutes."

"Ummm, no, tha fuck I can't."

"Don't leave from in front of that mother fuckin' house!" Big Worm barked the order through clenched teeth, his tone of voice hard and intimidating. Bunny gave him a stern look. He ended the video call before she could get out another word, closed his eyes, and waited a short while for the intense wave of teeth-clenching anger to dissipate. To further alleviate the fiery tension, he drew in a deep breath, fully inflating his one good lung, and held it in for a few seconds before exhaling heavily.

To put it mildly, Big Worm liked Bunny; to be more precise, he loved her. But the fact remained that he was a high-ranking gang member, a millionaire, drug dealer, a dark force of criminality that had never killed a person himself but had paid top dollar for the killings of several men who'd played with his money over the years. The streets of Chicago had hardened him, turned his heart to bone. There was a time when Worm had cared deeply for others, but that time had long since passed. Now he only cared about his money—particularly the $5,075,000 that had taken him almost three whole days and nights to count up and rubber-band and pack into the suitcases.

If Bunny let the woman whose name she'd learned was Whitney Clarrett get away from that house without following her, Worm feared he might catch his very first body.

"We caught up with buddy who shot you a couple hours ago," Bam said, pulling Worm from his reverie. "He in the air somewhere. The lil' bros took his head off."

Worm gave a barely discernible nod, the corners of his mouth rising in satisfaction. "Good. Good." He opened his eyes and checked his smartphone for the time: 1:25 p.m. He nodded again. "How much you pay for the hit?"

"A hun'ed thousand. Plus, another ten piece I paid a bitch for the location."

"I'm paying you back every dollar when we get back home. I still got a hun'ed racks and three bricks of dog put up." Worm absentmindedly stroked the rough exterior of the cast on his left arm.

"Man, I don't give a fuck about that money." Bam glanced over at Worm. "I found the nigga who shot my brother and got him stretched. That's what I'm supposed to do."

Worm shrugged his right shoulder, because shrugging both would have undoubtedly brought on another ache. "Still paying you back. That boy could've killed me. What was his name?"

"Eric. They called him Wack-a-Man."

Worm chuckled once at this. "Wack-a-Man, huh?" He turned stiffly toward Bam, looking his brother in the eyes. "Thanks, bruh. On Pops, as soon as we get this money back, I'm taking you straight to the A and linking you with Freckles. I'm done with this shit."

Bam's expression brightened immediately. The smile that spread across his face showcased all of his diamond teeth and the alluring rainbow of colors that twinkled across them in the sunlight. He'd been trying for over two years to get Worm to plug him with Freckles, Worm's heroin plug. Freckles was a black man about Worm's age from the zone six area of Atlanta, Georgia. Bam had seen Freckles twice before, when Bam was in Atlanta with Worm, throwing thousands of dollars at the tirelessly twerking exotic dancers at Tootsies. Both times, they had returned back to Chicago the following morning with no less than ten bricks in the trunk, and Worm had cut the bricks several times over before selling them to Bam and other dealers all across the Midwest. Bam knew for certain that, if he had the plug to himself, he could easily see $20 million in a year's time. He'd told Worm this a hundred times in the past.

"Say no more," Bam said. He pressed down a little harder on the gas pedal. The numbers on the digital speedometer climbed to 88 mph.

Worm cracked a grin and nodded yet again. He had just given Bam all the motivation needed to assist him in recovering his millions, and as long as they succeeded in finding it, he would stick to his word and let Bam take his place in the business dealings with Freckles.

For a small fee, of course.

***

Bunny gritted her perfect teeth and pounded her fist against the lower curvature of her steering wheel. She had a large bag of *Flamin' Hot Cheetos*, a small bag of *Sour Skittles*, and a 20-ounce bottle of Pepsi in a plastic bag on the passenger seat, but she wanted something more filling—a burger, or a burrito, or *something*.

Fuck it, she thought, and reached for the Skittles. She was hot and hungry and pissed that she'd agreed to drive here in the first place. "Should've just kept my black ass in Chicago. But noooo. I wanted to go and check on *Worm's* fat ass. The same nigga who almost got me *killed* three months ago. The *hell* was I thinking?"

She scarfed down the candy, relishing the sweet and sour taste as she dumped generous helpings into her mouth and chewed. She cracked open her lukewarm Pepsi and took three long swallows. Cranked up the volume on Kodak Black's "Super Gremlin."

When she looked out toward Whitney's house again, she saw that someone had closed the front door.

"Breaking news!" Bunny announced sarcastically, holding an imaginary microphone up to her mouth. "The front door to Whitney Clarrett's home has been *shut!* I repeat: *the door is shut!*"

She did an overly dramatic mic drop, rolling her eyes and shaking her head incredulously. A minute later, with nothing to do but sit and wait, she picked up her iPhone to scroll through social media.

Bunny XXX had amassed an impressive following in the months since her official porn debut, so impressive that she'd been able to get all of her accounts verified. Her official Pornhub page had 2.7 million followers, just a hundred thousand less than her TikTok page, and she had close to four million followers on Instagram. A lot of her followers were women and gay men who looked to her for advice on orally pleasuring their men, as if she had some sort of master's degree in advanced cocksucking. Others were celebrities in their own right, like legendary adult film stars: Pinky XXX, Cherokee D'Ass, and Roxy Reynolds, and "Girls Trip" star Tiffany Haddish. Just last week, Denver Broncos running back Keondre Muck had slid in her DMs and invited her to spend the night with him and his sexy model girlfriend Yamima Elsmley at the obnoxiously spacious Miami Beach mansion he called his summer home, and she had spent half the night with his dick in her mouth and her pussy in his girlfriend's mouth. The following morning, courtesy of the $210 million his four-year contract guaranteed, Keondre had gifted her a white croc skin Hermes Birkin bag that set him back $90,000. He'd already messaged her again, this time suggesting she put her porn career on hold and move into his Denver mansion until football season started.

Super Gremlin

Bunny was seriously considering the proposition.

"So why in the fuck am I *here*?" She said it out loud, emphasizing to herself the absurd comparison between her wild night in Miami Beach last week and the sheer boredom of sweltering in ninety-degree temperatures while staking out some small town stranger's house today. "Fuck my life," she muttered, a somber note of finality darkening her tone.

She was swiping through the many comments under the last bikini-clad video she'd uploaded to Instagram when the boredom she'd been enduring for the past hour took a surprising turn.

Tires screeched from somewhere close by. Bunny looked up from her phone and watched in open-mouthed amazement as a red Honda sedan veered wildly off Michigan Boulevard, rounded the corner of the florist's shop, and sped toward the vacant parking space in front of the house Bunny was surveying, its front tires bumping up onto the curb. Four frantic teenagers—three cute light-skinned girls and a dark-skinned boy—spilled out of the car.

Bunny immediately saw what all the panicking was about. The boy was clearly injured. His head was lumped up in some places, swollen in others, and there was blood all over his face and the sky blue t-shirt that was torn halfway down his back. The girls helped him along as he stumbled through the chain link gate and bobbled up the concrete walkway to Whitney Clarrett's front porch. The scrawny boy made it onto the second step and then fell down hard and clumsily, a fall made worse by the youngest girl. The girl had been holding on to his waist to keep him balanced from behind, and when he went down, she went down with him, landing heavily on his back and driving his bony chest into the concrete steps.

The other two girls looked like identical twins in their skin-baring red booty shorts and white halter tops. The halters were spattered and smeared with blood.

"Mama! Mamaaa!" screamed one twin.

The second twin ran up the remaining steps and pounded her small fist on the door before trying to the doorknob and finding it unlocked. She threw open the door and screamed into the house; whatever she screamed was out of Bunny's earshot.

So Bunny lowered her window, not even minding the suffocating wave of heat that swept in as she did it, burning away the little coolness her air-conditioning provided.

Seconds later, the woman Bunny suspected was Whitney Clarrett stepped hurriedly into the open doorway, a plain white cotton robe wrapped around her curvaceous body, a shower cap on her head, water dripping from her notably attractive face.

The woman took hold of the boy's arm and helped him to his feet, looking him over as she and the three girls ushered him inside. Just before the door slammed shut, Bunny realized that the boy only wore socks on his feet, no shoes.

"What the fuck!" Bunny murmured.

She took another swallow of her soda and redialed Big Worm's phone number.

Chapter Eight

Whitney guided her son into the first-floor bathroom and sat him down on the toilet lid to assess his injuries. She dampened a towel and used it to staunch the blood flowing out of a deep laceration an inch above his left eyebrow, which she decided would need a few stitches. Both of his eyes were swollen; the left one almost completely shut. His nose had a little swelling and there was blood trickling out of both nostrils. Disguised behind his thin mustache was another deep, bleeding laceration. The right side of his upper lip was fat and split open, and a canine tooth on that side was missing its lower half. Whitney poked and prodded at his ribs and found that none were broken. He'd be okay. Whitney knew her way around an injury; she'd been a paramedic for seven years before leaving the medical field to start her cosmetics company.

The worry that had nearly brought Whitney to tears moments earlier faded away and was quickly replaced by a searing-hot rage. She clenched her teeth and flared her nostrils and forced herself not to scream as she searched through her iPhone's contacts and phoned Jhareka Marvell, a paramedic she'd worked alongside. For four years. Within seconds, she had an ambulance in transit to her address.

She looked down and scowled at a blood smear on the side of her robe. It was only a forty-dollar bathrobe she'd bought off Amazon, but she was pissed about it just the same. And she was naked under it. The shower was still running. Her outfit—a gray and white Fashion Nova catsuit to coordinate with the fly purple ensemble Markio was rocking—was folded on the straw lid of her clothes hamper.

She looked to her daughters; the three of them stared back at her with varying expressions on their pretty teenage faces. Joselyn had tears in her eyes as she stood beside her big brother, rubbing a consoling hand up and down his back. Ava sat on the edge of the bath tub with her back against the shower curtain, looking hopeless and upset, her mind clearly rattled by the fact that her notoriously overprotective brother now seemed to need protection of his own. And Eva, the hothead of the trio, stood leaning back against the sink with her arm crossed over her chest and the side of her mouth raised in a malevolent snarl.

"What the hell happened?" Whitney asked, speaking to no one in particular.

"I got jumped," said Lil Jimmy. "Me and Crystal was walking through the apartments when—"

"Which apartments?" Whitney interjected. "And why were you walking? Where is our car?"

"Southgate Apartments," Lil' Jimmy elaborated. "I had just parked my car in the parking lot across from Crystal's building. She was about to go in and get a bathing suit so we could go to the beach. As soon as we got out of the car and started walking toward her apartment, a dark blue Charger whipped up in front of us. Some older dude yelled out the window at me, asked me if I was your son. I said yeah, and they got out and jumped me."

Ava said, "They knocked him out, Mama, and they posted the video on Facebook. Some boy named James from Harborside posted it on his page. A lot of our friends who saw it sent us clips and screenshots of the video. That's how we knew where to find him."

Lil' Jimmy leaned forward, holding the bloodied towel to the gash in his forehead, looking straight down at his blood-spotted Jordan socks. "They took my shoes, Mama. the J's you just got me last month." He shook his horribly battered head and exhaled a great sigh of defeat. "They embarrassed me in front of my girl."

"Fuck that bitch!" Eva snapped. "You got jumped on by four different niggas and she didn't even help! Where the fuck was *she* at when them niggas was—"

"Eva!" Whitney narrowed her eyes at the irate teen and spoke very slowly. "Watch your mouth, Eva. Don't get fucked up in here. I know you're upset, but I'm standing here in front of you. Show me some respect. And go out there and park my car the right way before you mess around and get it towed."

Eva stormed out of the bathroom, her footsteps as thunderous as Sasquatch feet as she passed through the house.

Quietly, Ava said, "She ain't letting Crystal off the hook this time. You know how much she already hates that girl."

Whitney only sighed and shook her head. Her smartphone rang with a call from Black Jimmy, but she hardly even noticed it. Her mind was stuck on what had happened to her son.

She knew who owned the blue Dodge Charger. It was Veezo's old friend Gregory Samuels, also known as G-Money, a Gangster Disciple from some Chicago suburb who'd traveled to Michigan City in 2014 with plans to take over the local drug trade. For a few years he had seen a certain level of success, enough to buy some nice cars and jewelry for himself and several of his young dealers, enough to buy his way into the hearts and panties of every gullible young that knew of him. But all good things eventually came to an end, and his turn came in the spring of 2018 when a drug task force raided his trap houses. He'd been convicted of dealing cocaine to a confidential informant and sentenced to nine years in the Indiana Department of Corrections. Whitney knew that G-Money had somehow gotten out of prison early—Candace had seen him at Walmart four days ago, and she'd called Whitney right away—but she hadn't expected him to be so upset over Veezo's death that he would attack one of her children.

"Black Jimmy's calling me now," she said finally, handing her phone to Lil' Jimmy. "Here. Talk to your father in the kitchen. I'm about to get dressed. Joselyn, go in my room and fetch my gun from out of that bottom drawer. Put it into the purse I left on my dresser and bring me the purse."

When Lil' Jimmy and Joselyn were gone, Whitney turned to Ava. "G-Money did this. He's one of your father's old friends. I guess he's mad about what happened."

"Well," Ava said decidedly, "he's a coward for putting his hands on a teenager just like my daddy was a coward for putting his hands on a woman."

Ava's positive spin on the situation did little to brighten her mother's troubled disposition. Mainly because Whitney was pretty sure Ava would feel differently about her father if she knew the true cause behind the death.

Whitney rinsed the blood from her hands and got dressed quickly, and instead of the Jimmy Choo platform pumps she'd planned to wear with her catsuit, she opted for plain white Air Force Ones, the official "fighting shoes" of the hood.

She was ready to go when the ambulance arrived minutes later. She and the girls would load into her Honda and follow behind the ambulance, and Black Jimmy would meet them at the hospital.

Descending the porch steps behind her daughters, Whitney looked past the ambulance to the red Range Rover parked across the street. She cocked her head a little to the side. Furrowed her brow. Squinted.

The girl behind the wheel was watching her.

The driver of the Range Rover looked away, but Whitney was certain the girl had been staring right at her, with a smart phone held up so that the rear camera lens faced Whitney's house. Whitney had noticed the conspicuous SUV when

Markio dropped her off less than an hour ago, but she hadn't really looked at it until now.

Feigning ignorance, Whitney walked to her car as the medics loaded Jimmy into the back of the ambulance. She didn't speak until she and the girls were seated in the Accord.

"Y'all ever seen that red truck before?"

The three teens turned to look out the driver's side windows, and from the backseat Joselyn said, "No, but I think she took pictures or video of us when we walked out of the house."

"Yeah," Whitney said, turning her key in the ignition, "I thought that, too."

***

Whitney wasn't the only one feeling watched.

As Markio counted through the mound of cash he'd made from exotic weed sales, he could feel Mya's deliberate gaze on the side of his face.

He was parked in his sister's driveway with Mya in the passenger seat next to him, her left leg folded beneath her in the seat, her body turned to face him. She had slipped the shoe of her left foot—a small tan-colored ankle boot with vertical green-and-red stripes down the sides—and let it drop into the footwell. She was wearing designer shorts again, only this time they were tan-colored with Gucci's signature double-G logo printed all over them. The same design and color scheme graced her stylish visor cap and the skin-tight T-shirt she wore over her obviously braless breasts.

"You know, you're pretty handsome for a man your age," Mya said

Markio cracked up laughing. "What? My age? What the fuck is that supposed to mean?"

"It means you're old. I looked you up. When you got arrested for murder sixteen years ago, the newspaper article said you was nineteen. I was nineteen *two* years ago, and you was nineteen *sixteen* years ago. That makes you thirty-five, which is basically forty. But it's cool, though. Old niggas is in. Y'all the ones doin' all the trickin', and *all* you old niggas eat pussy. Y'all winnin'." When Markio didn't reply, she added, "So you make good money selling weed out here?"

He nodded , folding the cash and stuffing it down into the left-hand pocket of his jeans. He'd made four other sales before driving here to meet up with Mya. Two of the sales were two-hundred-dollar plays, and Mya had just paid him $800 in crisp new blue-faced hundreds. "Yeah, I do a'ight. I just made fourteen hundred in the past thirty minutes. What do you do? I *know* you make good money."

Mya sucked her teeth. "You don't know shit."

"I know that G-Wagon you got parked over there cost two hundred thousand. I know you keep paying me with these brand new hundreds."

"For the record, my brother bought me that truck." She brought the baggie containing the ounce of gelato she'd just purchased up to her nose, closed her pretty eyes, and inhaled the potent aroma. "But yes, I do make good money. I'm a realtor. One of the top realtors in the region, actually. In the top five percent."

"Aw, that's what's up. I might need you to help me buy a crib one of these days. I just moved into a new house yesterday, but I'm only renting. I wanna own a house. Might move back to the city, though. I ain't decided yet."

"What city?"

"Chicago. That's where I'm originally from."

Mya gasped. "Are you serious?" She slipped off her other Gucci boot and kneeled in her seat facing him. "Where at in

Chicago? Yo' from out south somewhere, ain't you? Where you from? Roseland? Englewood?"

Markio gave her a stone-faced look.

"Out east?" She prodded.

"Nah. I'm from out west. I was born in the Rockwell buildings, but I grew up with the Travelers on 15th and Trumbull."

"*Aaahh!*" Mya screeched. She threw herself at Markio and wrapped her arms around his neck. He laughed out loud as she tightened her embrace, her closeness flooding his nose with the sweet scent of her perfume.

"What the fuck is wrong with you?" Markio asked with a light chuckle. "You a'ight, lil' mama?"

"I know who you are," Mya said, pulling back a little. "I *knew* you looked familiar. We're from the same neighborhood. I wasn't even born when y'all moved out here, but I've seen pictures of you at Miss Carolyn's house, and I remember seeing these 'Free Kio' shirts Kay had everybody wearing. You're Miss Carolyn's nephew, right? Hove's cousin?"

Markio looked at Mya with his mouth open in disbelief.

Then his heart swelled with emotion and a warm smile came to his face as he thought of his cousin Joseph Rice, whose nickname had naturally evolved from J.O.E. to J-Hova and finally to Hove. sadly, Hove had died of a drug overdose in 2017. Hove and his three younger brothers had practically raised Markio, looking after him while Markio's mother Jeanette ran the streets with her friend Margerie. Hove was Aunt Carolyn's oldest son, and just like Hove, every single one of Carolyn's sons was a gang member. Hove had been a Mafia Insane Vice Lord: the brother directly under him in age, Huey, was a Black Gangster New Breed; and the two youngest brothers, Kay and Buck, were Traveling Vice Lords. Markio was just seven years old when he became a Traveler, and his hot temper and fearless disposition had quickly earned him the gang's respect. Although mama had packed up and moved her kids to Michigan City when Markio was eight, he had never gone more than a week or two without returning to his old neighborhood, often spending weekends and entire summers at Aunt Carolyn's.

And the gang mentality had never really left him.

"Don't look so surprised," Mya said, stuffing the bag of weed down into her Gucci shoulder bag. "I've met a lot of people out here from the city. Just never expected to meet somebody from out my way. You grew up around my big brothers."

"Your big brothers?"

Mya nodded and was opening her pretty mouth to speak when Markio's phone rang. He looked down at his iPhone—it lay screen-up on the center console, connected to the phone charger—and saw that it was Whitney calling. The number popped up as "Wifey."

"Well, I know what that means," Mya said, and before Markio could respond, she pushed open the passenger door. "I'll take that as my cue to leave."

She leaned forward to slip on her ankle boots, her shirt inching up her back as she did it. A tattoo began on the left side of her lower back and continued around to her ribcage. It depicted a beautiful black mermaid, her tail turquoise in color, her top half a shade darker than Mya's reddish-brown complexion. The mermaid had a fat round ass like the woman she was tatted on, and one perky titty was exposed as she lugged a large brown Gucci bag by the straps, a bag that was overflowing with hundred-dollar bills.

Markio wanted badly to see the rest of the tattoo. He reached toward Mya, intent on lifting her shirt up even further, but he resisted the temptation and instead picked up his phone.

He answered the FaceTime call just as Mya hopped out of the truck; her fat booty jiggled as she landed on the gravel driveway outside. She dug a wedgie out from between her butt cheeks as she pushed the door shut. Out of the corner of his eye he saw Whitney's face on his phone screen, but he didn't take his eyes off Mya's bouncy round ass as she ran across Nissa's grass lawn and up the porch steps. In fact, if not for the sound of Whitney in distress, Markio might have watched Mya until she disappeared into the house.

But his eyes darted to the phone screen as soon as he heard the familiar sniffling that always accompanied Whitney's crying fits. He saw the tears streaming down her distraught face and immediately felt a pang of regret for lusting after Mya when his own beautiful queen was somewhere crying without him.

"Baby, what's wrong?" he said.

Whitney only glanced at Markio. In that fleeting glance he saw a barely contained rage permeating from her bloodshot eyes. She kept staring at something off-screen.

"You better come bond me out," she said. "You better fuckin' come bond me out, because I'm about to go *straight* to fuckin' jail."

"*What*? Wait, wait, wait. What the fuck happened?"

"G-Money and three other bitch-ass niggas jumped my son, and now he got some bitch following me. It's the same red Range Rover that was parked across the street when you dropped me off. The bitch was recording a video of me when I walked out the house. My son just got taken to the hospital in an ambulance, and that ho followed my car all the way here. I'm about to walk out there, snatch that bitch out of that Range Rover, and stomp her motherfuckin' ass through the ground."

"Walk out where?" Markio asked.

"To the parking lot. I'm sitting here in the *Emergency Room*, in the little waiting area or whatever the fuck they call it, and I can see the bitch sitting in the Range Rover from here."

"Which G-Money you talking about? Greg?"

"What other fuckin' G-Money yo' know?" Whitney snapped, her furious red eyes flashing at Markio.

"Baby, calm down." He started his SUV and threw it in reverse. "Tell Lil' Jimmy to say he don't know who jumped him when the detectives come in there. Leave that shit in the streets. I'll be there in a few minutes, a'ight? Just wait for me, and don't do shit till I get there. Can you do that for me?"

Whitney was quiet for a long moment. Markio could tell by the way the camera was shaking that her legs were bouncing uncontrollably, something she always did just before she lost her temper and stomped a bitch through the mother fucking ground.

"No," she said finally. "No, fuck that. You're on parole. You won't be able to bond out if you get locked up, but I can. So bond me out."

And with that she ended the call.

Chapter Nine

Bunny both felt and heard her stomach growl out in protest of her involuntary hunger strike. She delivered a frustrated punch to her dashboard, then slouched forward and rested her forehead on the steering wheel.

"Fuck you, Worm," she muttered weakly.

She knew that it was ultimately her bad spending habits that had landed her in this predicament. Sure, she made hundreds of thousands of dollars doing what she did, especially from her OnlyFans account, but the money was gone as fast as it came. She had a million-dollar wardrobe that included more than a hundred and fifty pairs of designer shoes. Just yesterday she'd purchased two Hermes Birkin bags—a green one and the pink one she had with her now—that cost her more than thirty thousand dollars each. She'd paid $87, 500 cash for the Range Rover and $91, 900 for her white Corvette, and her credit card debt now exceeded three hundred thousand dollars.

The available balance in her Chase Bank account was $2, 212.14.

So yes, she did need the $50,000 Worm had offered her to track down the buyer of his storage locker; needed it quite badly, in fact. But she hated the covert spying she had to do to get it. There had been one frightening moment outside Whitney Clarrett's residence when Bunny thought she'd been seen. She had watched Whitney pause mid-stride and look right at her. In that instant, Bunny had dropped her phone and looked away, her heart pounding at her ribcage as if it were trying to find a way out, but when she looked back a few seconds later Whitney and the three teenage girls were piling into the red Honda.

Now she was no longer worried about being discovered. Worm and his gang would be here soon. The text message he'd sent her five minutes ago said he was fifteen minutes away. As soon as he arrived, Bunny was leaving. She'd collect her $50,000 later on, when Worm returned to Chicago. She was done with Michigan City, Indiana.

She lifted her head off the steering wheel to look at her diamond Cartier wristwatch (another gift from Worm) for the time—just as her driver door swung open.

Her eyes widened in surprise, and she looked out the door at Whitney Clarrett and one of the twin girls just as the two of them reached in and dragged her out of the Rover.

**

Whitney closed her hand around the front of the girl's slender neck while Eva took hold of the girl's arm, and together they pulled her struggling body out of the SUV.

"You wanna follow *me*?" Whitney screamed and punched the girl twice in the face.

Eva had fists of fury. The sixteen-year-old's punches slammed fast and hard, pummeling the girl's face so speedily that Whitney found it impossible to land a punch of her own until the girl in the hot-pink dress crumpled to the ground. That's when Whitney started raining blows all across the back and sides of the girl's cowering head as the girl began screaming for help.

"Naah, bitch. Ain't no fuckin' help," Whitney said in between blows. "The next time you let G-Money send you out on a dummy mission, make sure you remember this." She kicked the girl in the face, and blood began to pour down onto the pavement as the girl struggled on her hands and knees.

"I don't—know a G-Money," the girl said, spitting out a mouthful of blood. "I swear, I—"

Eva grabbed the girl by the hair and lifted her head. There was a lot of blood gushing out of the girl's mouth and nose, and one eye was beginning to swell.

"You swear what, bitch?" Eva asked.

"It's the—storage locker. That's it. I swear. I never heard of no G-Money. I'm getting fifty thousand for finding out who—who bought the locker."

Whitney gasped and silently mouthed, "Oh, shit." Eva looked at her, still holding the girl by the hair.

"What is she talking about, Mama? What storage locker?"

"Shit," Whitney muttered. "I need to call Markio. Let her go. Come on. We gotta go."

But as she turned toward the emergency room entrance, she saw that several people who'd stepped outside for a smoke were watching her, their eyes and mouths agape. One woman had her smartphone out and was recording video. And a military-looking white man was running toward Whitney, holding a walkie-talkie up to his mouth with one hand and a pair of handcuffs in the other. Whitney knew that the police department usually kept plain-clothes detectives on patrol inside the hospital, not only to keep the staff and patients safe from potential threats but also to question the victims of violent crimes.

There was no sense in trying to run. Whitney turned away from the quickly approaching officer and put her hands behind her back. Seconds later, the handcuffs slammed down around her wrists.

***

The flashing red-and-blue lights of seven Michigan City Police Department vehicles was the first thing Markio saw when he pulled into the parking lot at St. Anthony's Hospital.

"Shit, Whitney," he said, slowing his SUV to a crawl as he drove toward the chaos. He couldn't afford to draw any undue attention. He still had a year of parole left to do, and he had a Glock with an extended magazine under his seat. Not to mention the more than two ounces of gelato he had in the back.

The police had Whitney and either Ava or Eva (Markio still had a hard time telling the twins apart) leaning forward against an MCPD patrol car with their hands cuffed behind them, while ten feet away two nurses attended to a brutally battered young brown-skinned woman in a blood-soaked pink dress. The woman was sitting in a pool of blood next to the open driver door of the cherry colored Range Rover.

Markio found a vacant parking space near Whitney's car and pulled into it. Whitney's other two daughters had been standing amongst a small crowd of spectators outside the emergency room doors, and they quickly walked over to his truck as he opened his door and stepped out.

"Why didn't y'all try to stop her?" he asked them.

"You know ain't no stoppin' Mama," Joselyn said, looking back at her mother as the police were shoving Whitney into the back seat of an MCPD squad car. "Once she sets her mind on something, she does it. And if it's something violent, Eva's jumping in with her."

"I should've known that was Eva," Markio said, watching as Eva was placed in the back of a different patrol car. "I told Whitney to wait for me."

"She yelled something to me after that undercover cop handcuffed her," Ava said. She had Whitney's purse hanging down from one shoulder. Markio could tell from the redness in her eyes that she'd been crying. "At least I *think* he was undercover. He wasn't wearing a police uniform like the other police."

"What did she say?"

"She said to tell you to check the suitcases."

The suitcases? Markio thought. *She's on her way to jail, and she's still thinking about those stupid-ass suitcases?*

He turned toward the police cars, and for a long time he stared at the squad car Whitney was seated in. He didn't think of the suitcases. He thought of Whitney's bond, wondering how much it would cost him and how soon he'd be able to post it. He thought of the potential charges—aggravated battery, battery with serious bodily injury.

"I'll drive the car home after they release Jimmy," Ava said. "Black Jimmy was supposed to meet us here, but he ain't showed up yet. I just talked to Auntie Candace. She's on her way here now."

Markio crossed his arms over his chest and leaned back against his truck, thinking. After a moment he sighed and said, "I don't want y'all staying at home tonight. Either stay the night at my house or stay with Candace. I don't know what's goin' on but I don't think it's a good idea for y'all to go home if this nigga G-Money got people watching the house."

"We'll stay with Aunt Candace," Ava said.

Markio nodded in agreement, and when Ava's eyes filled with tears as the cars holding her mother and sister rolled away a minute later, he put an arm around her shoulders and pulled her close. She pressed her face into his shirt and cried. He rubbed her back and told her it would be okay. Markio may not have had any children himself, but he loved Whitney's as if they were his own. His heart ached for them when they were sad, and quite often he took their side when they were mad.

"Y'all go on back in there and wait on Lil' Jimmy," he said, after some time. "I'm about to go find this nigga G-Money and see what's up. I'll Cashapp the money to Candace when they give your mama a bond. She should be home in an hour or two."

Sniffling, Ava nodded and took a step back. She put on a weak smile, wiped her face, and followed Joselyn back into the hospital.

Markio got in his Mercedes truck and slowly reversed out of the parking spot. There were still five police cars parked nearby, and he didn't want to give them any reason to look his way. The only person he was looking to give some trouble to this hot July afternoon was Gregory "G-Money" Samuels.

Driving out of the hospital parking lot, Markio passed three blacked-out vehicles that were pulling *in* to the parking lot. The first vehicle, and SUV, caught his eye and caused him to do a double take as it cruised past the driver's side of this truck.

"Get the *fuck* outta here," he murmured in disbelief.

He'd never seen a Rolls-Royce Cullinan up close before.

Chapter Ten

Bam glanced over at Worm and shook his head. "High-ass nigga," he said, and chuckled. The roxies Worm had popped just as they hit the highway had him nodding in and out of consciousness. Right now he was in the "out" phase.

Bunny's red Range Rover was parked at the west end of the parking lot, right where five police cars sat with their emergency lights flashing, so Bam parked at the opposite end and dialed her phone number. He got no answer, even after redialing her number twice more.

He buzzed down his window when Pee Wee and Baby Lord appeared outside his door.

"What's the word, Lord?" Baby Lord asked.

"I'm thinkin'." Bam used an elbow to nudge Worm awake. "Bruh, getcho high ass up. We here at the hospital, and your girl ain't pickin' up the phone."

It took Worm a couple of seconds to shake off the drowsy effects of the drug. He looked over at Bam and the two Lords standing outside Bam's open window. Pee Wee's dreads had grown longer since the night Worm was shot, and he'd colored the tips of them blond. Worm had no idea who the other young man was, but he'd seen him once before, at a house party his little sisters had thrown on 15th and Haman Avenue back in February.

"Joe, I think she got beat up or some'n," Pee Wee said, shooting a glance in the direction of the police cars. "The driver door to that Range Rover was wide open, on fo'nem, and it's two nurses right there helpin' somebody."

Worm rubbed his hand down his face and sat forward. "In that last FaceTime call, I watched the red Honda she was fol-lowing pull into this parking lot and park right over there by the Emergency Room. Now I need one of y'all to walk over and see if it's still there. If it is, park somewhere close to it and watch that car. We'll leave one car here and the other car can follow us. We all don't need to be here. She ain't got no eight suitcases in that lil' bitty ass Honda. They're in that house on Comb Street."

"So why follow her?" Pee Wee asked. "We can just run in her crib and take the shit. On fo'nem, we ain't even gotta wait. I'll run straight in that bitch."

Worm was shaking his head, by way of saying: *No.* "We need to watch her just in case she stashed the suitcases somewhere else. We might have to snatch her up and make her tell us where it's at."

Pee Wee and Baby Lord both nodded understandingly. Pee Wee moved closer to Baby Lord, slipped him a handgun—the fully-automatic Glock 25 that Bam had supplied him with—and walked off toward the west end of the parking lot, while Worm typed Whitney Clarrett's home address into Google Maps.

Bam sat adjusting his bevy of diamond-encrusted necklaces. Then he adjusted his five-hundred-thousand-dollar white diamond Patek Philippe wristwatch, and his three diamond Cartier bracelets. He'd stuffed the front packets of his black Amiri jeans with $80,000 in hundred dollar bills, forty grand to each pocket. His black cap, black shirt, and black-and-white sneakers were also made by Amiri. He had an additional $400,000 in hundreds piled up in a Louis Vuitton duffle bag in the Cullinan's rear storage compartment. He'd had $500,000 in the duffle, but he had paid Baby Lord for the hit on Eric Shaw.

Baby Lord returned to the driver's seat of the Hellcat he was driving, and Bam raised his window and waited for the air-conditioning to cool the interior of his Rolls-Royce again.

He stared at the cast on Worm's left arm and said, "How bad that shit hurt?"

"Can't even feel it now," Worm said. "Them two roxies knocked that pain right out." He looked down at the cast. It was blue in color, and half the family (as well as most of the gang) had scribbled their signatures all over it when they visited him in the hospital yesterday. "The bullet wounds healed up good. It's the surgery scars that hurt like a motherfucka. But like I said, shit, I can't feel nothin' now. Them roxies work like magic."

Bam's mind went to thoughts of the heroin plug, and he asked, "How much Freckles be charging you for them bricks?"

"Same price I charge you. Sixty-five thousand."

"Yeah, but you step on it first."

"I only put a one on yours. I put a two or a three on everybody else's and I charge them eighty. You get a way better deal."

Bam nodded and smiled and rubbed his hands together like Birdman as the numbers started tumbling through his head. He remembered the last road trip they'd taken to Atlanta. They had rented a Kia Telluride from Hertz for the drug run, and Bunny had followed them there in her snow-white Corvette. When they returned to Chicago the next day, Bunny had thirty kilos of heroin packed into the truck of her car. Which meant the three plain black duffle bags Worm had handed over to Freckles contained approximately $1,950,000. If Bam made that same deal with Freckles, and cut each kilo into four kilos, he'd have 120 kilograms of heroin. He could easily wholesale the bricks for $80,000 apiece and still come off with $9.6 million.

His mind was still reeling with seven-figure numbers when he spotted Pee Wee walking back. He lowered his window again, suddenly noticing that a collection of dark gray storm clouds had drifted out in front of the sun. From somewhere on the horizon, a stentorian clap of thunder boomed across the sky.

"Yeah, it's over there. A red Honda Accord," Pee Wee said. "The law just pulled off. I saw Bunny, too, and oowee, somebody beat the *brakes* off her ass. On fo'nem. Her whole face swollen. I'm about to pull up and park."

Bam nodded in agreement, and seconds later he cruised out of the hospital parking lot with one less Challenger Hellcat trailing behind him.

Chapter Eleven

"Folks, on Larry Bernard Hoover, as soon as the lil' nigga said his mama was the bitch who killed Folks, we got on his ass, G. stomped him out and everything," G-Money said proudly.

"But … but, man … but, man, y'all stomped out a kid," stuttered Lorenzo "Blubby" Chavis. He'd had the peculiar stutter all his life, and he'd never once been bullied over it. If anything, the bullies worried about being bullied by him. Blubby was a Gangster Disciple from Lakeland projects, though he claimed Dub Life, the west side clique he'd been racking with for years.

"Fuck that nigga," G-Money said. "Like I said, his mama killed Veezo. I'm on that with her and every nigga who fuck with her from now on. On fo' nam grave."

He sipped from his ice-cold bottle of beer as he stood with a small crowd of ten fellow Gangster Disciples behind a trap house near 7th Street and Willard Avenue, watching the dice game taking place on the concrete walkway in front of him and placing side bets every few rolls. They were in the backyard of a house that belonged to a GD called Sway Swanson and his brother Shannon. The trap house had grown so popular over the years that many west siders had started calling the entire block "7th Heaven."

"But … but, man, you know what?" Blubby tapped G-Money on one massively muscular arm, and when G-Money looked over at him he said, "I … I bet … I bet you ain't gon' try that G shit wit' Markio. You know that's his girl. Mar … Marki … but, man, Markio ain't no joke."

"Fuck that hook-ass nigga. He can get it too."

A frigid scowl formed on G-Money's dark-hued face. The term "hook" was a derogatory name for Vice Lords, a gang G-

Money had hated for as far back as he could remember. Growing up in Harvey, Illinois, he'd spent the majority of his teenage years at war with the conservative Vice Lords, the Four Corner Hustlers, and the Black P. Stones. Those bullet wars had taken the lives of his only brother, his closest cousin, and several GDs he'd grown up with, so now G-Money hated every gang under the umbrella of the five-pointed star. It didn't matter if they were Vice Lords, Black P. Stones, Four Corner Hustlers, or Latin Kings. As far as he was concerned, they were all opps, and opps were meant to be killed.

G-Money was built for the job. He was six feet four inches tall and two hundred fifty pounds of solid muscle. Intense weightlifting sessions during his first prison bid were responsible for his Herculean physique. He had done seven hard years at Menard Correctional Center in Illinois, at a time when it was considered the most dangerous prison in the state.

The black T-shirt G-Money wore had a photo of an incarcerated Larry Hoover, chairman and founder of the Gangster Disciples, printed on the front and the words "Free Larry Hoover" printed on the back. The shirt fit tightly on G-Money's powerful torso. The blue pair of Balmain jeans he wore was four years old but had never been worn. He'd paid five grand for the pair of designer jeans shortly before his 2018 arrest, when Balmain was the hottest fashion brand in the streets. The police had taken all of his cars and jewelry and most of his money, but his longtime girlfriend Janet McCoy had held onto his wardrobe.

She'd also held on to the 45-caliber Smith & Wesson pistol he had tucked in the front of his waistband.

Taking another swig from his beer, he thought about Markio, the Traveling Vice Lord who'd murdered a Black Disciple here in Michigan City a decade and a half ago. Word on the street was that Markio was a real savage, known for hopping out on niggas in broad daylight and opening fire. G-Money hadn't known anything about Whitney and Markio being together. That certainly changed things.

He swept his gaze around the small, barren backyard. Twenty feet behind him, a dull red shed stood just alongside the alleyway. There was a large, leafless tree a few feet to his right, a bunch of dead branches scattered around its base. He glanced into the alleyway. Looked beyond the alley to the next street over, where he knew Markio's sister Taquisha lived. He could see her house from where he stood, as well as her green Chevy Equinox sitting in the driveway.

Parked at the curb right in front of Taquisha's house was a compact white Mercedes-Benz SUV.

As if on cue, a crack of thunder rocked the darkening sky.

"It's about to start raining," Sway said, as he and the others looked up at the approaching storm clouds. "Come on, we'll go on the front porch."

G-Money took one last look back at the white Mercedes truck and briefly considered asking Blubby what kind of car Markio drove. "Man, fuck that hook-ass nigga," he repeated, waving off the thought and turning back to the gang.

Two seconds later, as he began to follow the others around the side of the house, he heard the sudden snap of a downed tree branch somewhere behind him. He looked back and found himself staring down the barrel of a Glock, held tight in the hand of a short, stocky man in a black ski-mask, a blue Colts hoodie, and gray jeans.

The gun flashed in G-Money's face, and he fell dead on the concrete walkway.

***

It hadn't taken much lurking on social media to pinpoint G-Money's location. Markio had just started tapping his way through the Instagram stories on his IG page when he found a short video his old friend Blubby had shared five minutes earlier of G-Money and some other guys at the 7th Street dice game.

Markio had been close with Shannon and Sway before he went to prison, and he was even closer with Blubby, who he'd known ever since he first set foot in Michigan City as a kid. He and Blubby had committed a hundred crimes together, everything from robbing businesses and stealing cars to selling crack and shooting guns.

Which was why Markio didn't shoot at the other Gangster Disciples who took off running after he shot G-Money through the face.

The bullet burned a perfectly circular dime-size hole just below G-Money's left eye. The exit wound created by the supersonic hollow-tipped round cratered the back of his skull, and he dropped like a sack of bricks. Markio stood over him just long enough to see that there was no chance of survival. Then he turned and ran.

He removed his mask as he crossed the alleyway, stuffing it and the Glock in the belly pocket of his hoodie. He was back in his truck and speeding off up 8th Street less than a minute after committing the murder.

Heart pounding, he made a number of sharp turns, speeding from one block to the next. By the time he heard the first scream of police sirens, he was fifteen blocks away from the scene of the crime, wrapping the gun and mask in the hoodie he'd taken from his nephew Tyquan's drawer and stuffing it down into the dumpster behind Patty's, a convenience store at the corner of 10th Street and Michigan Boulevard.

He climbed back into his truck with pure adrenaline coursing through him, and drove casually away, making the turn onto Michigan Boulevard and driving southbound, hardly even noticing the heavy downpour of rain that had started hammering his Benz from all sides. It had been a long time since he felt his heart beat as fiercely as it was beating now, and it only beat faster as two MCPD patrol cars shot past in the northbound lane. He took a second at the Vail Street red light to turn his phone back on, as he had shut it off before heading west. Then he drove to his new address, discretely parked his truck beneath the leafy limbs of a tree in his back-yard, and went inside to sit down on his new leather sofa and think.

He had just killed a man. It was the second murder he'd committed in Michigan City. The first had sent him away for *fifteen years*. But the previous one was different. Last time he'd had seven eyewitnesses fingering him as the shooter. This time there would be none, because he'd worn a mask. He'd looked at all the front porches and windows on 8th Street before he crossed the street and disappeared into the alleyway between 7th and 8th, and he'd seen no one. The men leaving the backyard dice game with G-Money had only seen a man wearing a ski-mask. That could've been anyone.

He lit a Newport cigarette and sucked in great lungfuls of the cancerous smoke, looking at a commercial for the upcom-ing *Black Adam* movie without really seeing it. Back in the day, when he was a ten-year-old troublesome kid living in one of the three roach-infested houses that had stood just over the fence from Lakeland projects, where he'd met his old friends Lil' Jack and Blubby. *The Rock* had been one of his favorite wrestlers, but right now he didn't give two fucks about The Rock's new movie.

He got up and went to his bedroom to change clothes, switching into a pair of red Jordan gym shorts, red-and-black Jordan 5 Retro sneakers, and a black wife beater.

He fell back onto the bed and stared up at his slowly spinning ceiling fan. "Shit," he muttered, and puffed on the cigarette as he considered the unnerving fact that he no longer had a firearm in his possession.

He sat up and logged into his Facebook app. Roughly one-third of the 2,212 people on his friends list were people he knew in Michigan City, and the rest were either his family and friends back home in Chicago or ex-cons and former correctional officers he'd met in prison.

A few seconds of scrolling was all it took to find what he was looking for. Anyssa Chavis, Blubby's older sister who lived right next door to Markio's sister Taquisha, had just posted a status confirming G-Money's passing:

'*Damn, RIP my nigga G-Money.*'

The post had already gotten fourteen sad reactions and three comments. '*G-Money from Harvey?*' And '*That is so sad.*' And '*Yeah your bro just called me saying G got killed on the side of Sway's house.*' The last comment was from Crystal Guy, another girl Markio knew from Lakeland projects.

There were several more posts about G-Money's death. Everyone was saying rest in peace and posting photos of G-Money on their pages.

After a moment's contemplation, Markio decided to post his own status update:

'*All this senseless violence needs to stop.*'

Two seconds later, his phone rang with a FaceTime call from Fat Jerm. He answered it and was immediately met by Jerm's questioning gaze. Jerm's eyes darted around, searching the background behind Markio.

"What's up, bruh?" Markio asked.

"Shite. I was callin' to let you know I returned the U-Haul for you. Drove it around for a lil' bit but I dropped it off with a full tank."

"Good lookin', bruh."

"You hear about G-Money?" Fat Jerm had an inquisitive look in his eyes when he asked the question.

Markio shrugged indifferently. "Yeah, I saw it on Facebook. But shit, fuck that nigga. He put his hands on my stepson earlier today. I ain't got no love for that clown-ass nigga."

"I already know. I just heard about that. I was just about to call you to see if you wanted me to check that nigga when I heard somebody smoked him." Jerm's fat bald head moved closer to the camera. "You ain't do that shit, did you?"

"Hell naw." Markio stood and headed for the bathroom. "I been in the crib chillin'. But like I said, fuck G-Money. Whitney just got locked up for whoopin' some bitch G-Money had following her. Matter of fact, let me let you go so I can call up to the jail and see if they gave her a bond yet."

After the call, Markio didn't call the jail. What he did do was stand at the bathroom sink and scrub his hands for three full minutes with Dove soap and Clorox bleach to get rid of the gunpowder residue that was undoubtedly all over his right hand and wrist. His phone rang again as he was drying his hands. He saw Crystal Guy's number and figured she might be calling to buy weed. He took the phone back to his bedroom and stood looking down at the designer clothes Whitney had left in neatly folded piles on the hardwood floor. Leaning his shoulder against the door frame, he answered the call.

"Yoooo," he said.

But no one spoke. All he heard was sniffling and sobbing on the other end.

"Hello?" he said.

"Hey, bro. This Crystal."

"I know who this is. What you cryin' for? Don't tell me it's about that bitch-ass nigga G-Money."

"No, no. Hell no. It's about Gabby."

Markio knew Big Gabby quite well. She was Crystal's niece, the fat little girl he'd fought and played around with in Lakeland projects, only now she was a much heavier grown woman, still as cool and funny as ever.

"What's wrong with Gabby?" he asked, glancing over at the eight steel suitcases next to his bed. *Naw, why in the hell did Whitney want me to check these dumbass suitcases*, he thought to himself.

"Here, I'll let her tell you," Crystal said, and seconds later Big Gabby was on the line. Markio could tell from how weak and shaky her voice sounded that she had been crying too.

"Hey, Markio."

"What's the word, my nigga?"

"I, umm—" She hesitated for a long moment. Markio took advantage of the pause in conversation to walk over and kick at the side of one of the suitcases. It didn't budge. "I've been sick as fuck lately," Gabby continued. "And when I went to see my doctor today they told me I, umm … I have cancer in my kidney."

"Damn," Markio said, and plopped down on the bed, the suitcases suddenly the furthest things from his mind. "I'm sorry to hear that, fam. That's some fucked up news."

"He said it's operable, but my health insurance won't cover the full cost of the surgery. I need to come up with *thirty-two thousand fuckin' dollars* to get the surgery, and that's just not somethin' I can do. I don't know how I'm gon' come up with that kinda money. Crystal started a GoFundMe, and so far we've raised about eighteen hundred. Anything you can afford to give will be highly appreciated. You know how much I hate askin' people for shit, but I have—"

"How soon can you get the surgery done?" Markio asked, cutting her off as he walked around the standing suitcases to his closet and pulled the backpack off the high shelf.

"I can get it done whenever I come up with the money."

"I got the money for your surgery, Gabby. I just wanna know how soon they can get you in surgery so you can get better."

Silence on the line again. Then whimpering. Sniffling. All out bawling. It went on like that for a while, with both Crystal and Gabby—and somewhere in the background, Gabby's teenage son—thanking him repeatedly as they cried tears of joy and gratefulness.

While they cried and thanked him, Markio dumped the cash from his backpack onto the heavy Louis Vuitton blanket on his bed and spent a lasting moment just looking at it, realizing he'd be giving up almost every dollar he had for Gabby's surgery. Not that he minded. There weren't many things in this world that Markio Earl enjoyed more than the soul-fulfilling act of helping others, especially single, struggling black mothers like Big Gabby. If he went broke doing it, then so be it.

King Rio

Chapter Twelve

"You didn't tell those detectives what happened, did you?"

Lil' Jimmy responded to Joselyn's question with an incredulous side-eye. "Come on now, sis. What the fuck I look like? Hell nah, I ain't tell them police *nothin'*. They asked me what happened and I said I don't know what happened, I got knocked out. Last thing I remembered was steppin' out of my car."

Joselyn let out a sigh of relief. She didn't know if she could live with her big brother being labeled a snitch. It would spread through their network of teenage friends on social media like a wildfire, and the kids at school would give them hell about it once summer break was over.

Aunt Candace only shook her head at the three of them—Joselyn, Ava, and Lil' Jimmy—as they walked out through the emergency room doors. She still had on her Olive Garden uniform. Her girlfriend—Tika—had planned a romantic spa date for the two of them to enjoy after Candace got off work, but unfortunately those plans had to be canceled. Candace's sister and one of her nieces were in jail; her only nephew had taken a serious beatdown from several adult men, and now there was word that the man responsible for the beatdown had been murdered.

The lesbian romance would have to wait.

"Dang, it's raining *hard*, ain't it?" Joselyn said, looking out into the steady downpour as they stopped beneath the awning just outside the automatic glass doors.

Candace stood there with her arms folded across her buxom chest, tapping the toe of her shoe on the dry slab of concrete. The rainfall had strengthened significantly since she first entered the *Emergency Room* twenty minutes ago, and the sky had become as dark as night. Blinding veins of lightning forked down from the black clouds every couple of seconds, the thunder racking the skies above.

"Why did I have to park so far off from this door?" Candace muttered.

Ava said, "Mama parked right there. "She pointed. "It's close. We'll just get in there and I'll drive you to wherever you parked." She didn't wait for an answer. She dug in her mother's purse, found the keys, and ran off into the rain, yelling out like the dramatic teen she was as the rain drenched her from head to toe.

While she watched her niece sprint to Whitney's car, Candace thought about the murder of Gregory "G-Money" Samuels and hoped to God it wasn't connected with her nephew's beating. Sure, she'd wanted to fuck G-Money up for hurting Jimmy, but she hadn't wanted him *dead*. She suspected that one of Jimmy's high school friends could be involved. Most of the boys Jimmy hung around were wannabe gangsters, influenced by the many rap stars they mimicked, celebrity gangsters: Lil' Durk, NBA YoungBoy, and EST Gee. One of Jimmy's teenage homies could have easily taken it upon himself to avenge Jimmy's beating.

Or was it someone else? Someone connected to Whitney. Someone like Markio.

Candace stuck out her bottom lip and squinted, thinking hard and staring vacantly into the falling rain as Ava started the Honda and slowly backed it out of the parking space.

Two spaces over from Whitney's car, the engine of a blacked-out Dodge Challenger roared to life.

Lil' Jimmy turned to Joselyn and asked, "Why did Eva and Mama jump that girl? You say she was following y'all?"

Joselyn nodded. "Yeah. The red truck that was parked across the street from the house when we brought you home. The girl was recording us, and she followed us here."

"She *recorded* you?" Candace tilted her head forward, her brow knitted in confusion as she pondered the unnerving incident. *Why on earth would someone be watching Whitney and her family so closely?*

She was still pondering the question when her smartphone began to ring. She answered it and heard a computerized voice: "You have a collect call from Whitney—an inmate at the Laporte County Jail. To accept this call, press zero."

Ava pulled up and reached across the passenger seat to push the door open for her aunt. Candace hit zero to accept the collect call, then ran the few feet to the open door and jumped in, while Lil' Jimmy and Joselyn rushed into the backseat.

"My bond is twenty-five hundred," Whitney said immediately. "They already moved me to the county jail. Tell Markio to come and get me right the fuck now and tell him to open those suitcases we got from the storage auction. I think it might be something value in one of them."

Candace wiped the rain from her face and put the call on speaker. "He told Ava to have me call him when they give you a bond and he'll send me the money. I'll text him now." She began texting the bond amount to Markio.

"They took Eva to the Juvenile Detention Center in Larporte," Whitney said. "She'll probably have to go to court sometime tomorrow before they release her."

"Everybody knows where JDC is, Mama," Joselyn said, just to be heard.

"Love you, Ma!" Lil' Jimmy shouted.

"What did they say at the hospital?" Whitney asked.

"I got five stitches above my eye, two in my lips, and three in the back of my head. They had to shave some hair off the back of my head to do the stitches. Other than that, I'm good. The swelling went down a bunch, too."

The audible *ching* of money hitting Candace's Cash App account alerted her to the money transfer from Markio. She checked it and saw that exactly $2,500 had just been deposited. When she looked up from her phone, she glanced over at the pitch black Dodge Challenger. It had backed out of its parking space and turned so that the front of it faced the hospital—faced Whitney's little red Honda—and now it sat idling twenty feet away.

"Did you hear about G-Money?" Candace asked, her eyes asquint as she regarded the Challenger with a critical stare.

"Hear what?" Whitney said.

"Girl, somebody killed him. It's all over Facebook. They say the shooter had a mask on when he popped out of the alley behind Sway and Shannon's house on 7th Street. He ran up and shot G-Money in the head. Nobody's saying who did it."

"*Wow*," was all Whitney could say. She drew out the word for three whole seconds

The low growl of the Dodge Challenger's muscular engine was gnawing at Candace's nerves. She had a terrible, gut-twisting feeling about that car.

"Markio just sent me the money," she said, studying the Challenger out of the corner of her eye so as not to alarm the teens. "I'll be there to get you in thirty minutes. I would say twenty but it's storming hard out here."

"Okay. Shit, that's crazy. Yeah, just come and get me." Whitney seemed shaken by the news of G-Money's murder. Candace wondered if her sister was thinking what she herself was thinking, that Markio might be the shooter.

The computerized voice came on again: "Thank you for using GTL."

Candace sat looking at her phone a second longer. Then she looked out into the relentless rainfall, eyeing the Challenger and thinking, thinking, thinking.

"Where did you park?" Ava asked.

"Right back there." Candace pointed a shaky forefinger in the direction she'd parked—roughly ten paces beyond the spot where the Challenger had been parked.

Ava spun the steering wheel all the way to the left and pressed down on the gas pedal, turning sharply toward the idling Challenger and driving straight toward it.

As they passed within inches of the ominous dark muscle car, Candace tried hard to peer in through the windshield, but the rain was coming down too hard to see anything beyond the windshield, and the driver's side windows were too darkly tinted. Still, she could almost feel the driver's eyes on her skin, warm and wet and sinister. It gave her goose bumps.

In the back seat, Jimmy was on his phone, talking with his girlfriend, Crystal Mitchell, who had apparently been chased off after Jimmy was knocked unconscious. Joselyn was busy texting friends and scrolling through social media. Ava, a rookie driver with only a learner's permit, was concentrating on her driving. Only Candace seemed to notice the blacked-out Dodge Challenger.

She looked back and wasn't surprised to see that it was making a U-turn.

"What the—?" She mouthed it silently as she attempted to slow her breathing. *Calm down*, she told herself. *Just calm down and breathe.*

Ava pulled to a stop behind Candace's ten-year-old Chrysler 300C.

"Follow me to the jail," Candace said.

"We need to go home and change first," said Ava. "We got Jimmy's blood all over our clothes. And he needs to change too."

"Hell yeah," Lil' Jimmy agreed. A nurse had given him a t-shirt embroidered with the St. Anthony's logo over the left breast, but his jeans were stained with blood and torn down the inner thigh.

"Nope." Candace was shaking her head. "All that can wait. Follow me to the county jail to get your mama out. Nobody's going back to that house until we figure out what's going on."

Ava sighed defeatedly, and Candace threw open her door and ran to her Chrysler, dialing 9-1-1 as she went.

***

Big Worm had two FaceTime video feeds on his phone screen at once, in split screen mode: live video of Pee Wee following close behind Whitney Clarrett's red Honda Accord, and a second live feed that showed Baby Lord and three more Vice Lords breaking into Whitney Clarrett's home to search for the suitcases.

It was like watching a virtual-reality video game. He watched in first-person as Baby Lord's black-and-gold Dior sneaker kicked open the front door. The camera rushed inside, a Glock with a 50-round drum magazine held out in front of it, and Big Worm saw what he decided was a nice single-family home. The living room gave off a sophisticated feminine vibe, with two-toned red-and-pink curtains over the windows, a fuchsia-colored sectional sofa and matching armchairs on a clean hardwood floor, a box of Kleenex tissues and a lidded crystal bowl filled with Reese's Peanut Butter cups on a glass-top coffee table, and a large screen television hanging on the wall. One of the first-floor bedrooms obviously belonged to a teenage girl, as evidenced by the Pooh Shiesty poster with lipstick kiss marks planted all over it and the volleyball trophies on the dresser. Baby Lord and the other three Lords tossed the room, ripping out drawers and flipping the bed. They found nothing.

The next first-floor bedroom was the master, and there were clear signs that it belonged to Whitney Clarrett, namely the stack of mail on the dresser with her name printed on each envelope. Baby Lord snatched out all nine drawers and dumped them on the floor, finding nothing other than a bunch of nice-looking women's clothing, a box of 9-millimeter ammunition, and a massive ebony dildo. He flipped the queen-size mattress of the neatly made bed and found nothing underneath it. Looked under the bed and saw nothing aside from four pairs of designer shoes and an empty Magnum condom wrapper. Searched her closet and found only more of her shoes and clothes.

Down in the basement, there seemed to be some sort of in-home lip gloss business in operation, with racks of iKiss merchandise taking up half the floor space and flattened cardboard boxes for packaging and shipping piled atop a foldable wooden table against one cinder block wall.

On the second floor, there were three more bedrooms, as well as a second bathroom and a lined closet. The gang ransacked them all, even going as far as to search the attic, the kitchen, and the first-floor bathroom.

But there were no signs of the eight steel suitcases. Nor were there any clothes-filled trash bags or any of the other things Worm had stored in his storage locker, and this made Big Worm's blood boil.

He dropped the phone onto his lap and pounded his fist on the dashboard. Bam looked over and gave him a hard look.

"Ay, man. Punch on your own shit," Bam said.

Big Worm's "own shit" was parked right in front of Bam's Cullinan—a pearl-white Rolls-Royce Phantom on 24-inch white-painted Forgiato rims.

They were parked in the horseshoe-shaped driveway in front of a lakefront mansion that had cost their mother $2.1

million to purchase. Behind the 7,100-square foot mansion's vast back lawn, Lake Michigan's dazzling blue waters extended for as far as the eye could see. Jesse Mae had legally purchased the estate using the money from her deceased husband's two-million-dollar life insurance policy and the seven-figure income she received from Golden Express, the trucking company she and her brother—Milton "Fats" Lee—owned. Aunt Rina managed the Chicago-based company, and Worm's two oldest sons had gotten their CDLs just to join the lucrative family business.

"Chill the fuck out, bruh," Bam said, lighting a Backwoods cigarillo he had just stuffed with black cherry gelato. He puffed on the exotic strain and sipped from a double-stacked 7-Eleven gas station cup he'd filled with ice, Sprite soda, and Actavis promethazine with codeine syrup. "We ain't got nothin' but time. That lil' bitch gon' run us that bread. Either that or she gon' watch her whole family die. I doubt she'll choose that route."

Big Worm was too furious to speak, so he said nothing. He picked his phone back up. Baby Lord had ended his video call, but Pee Wee's was still going. The thunderstorm was beginning to let up, both here by the lake and wherever Pee Wee was driving. The rainfall faded to a light drizzle, and the dark clouds began to separate, allowing the sun to show its scorching hot forehead.

Worm saw a flash of red inside Pee Wee's car. At first he thought his eyes were playing tricks on him. Then he realized they weren't.

Pee Wee said, "Aw, shit. That's twelve back there. On fo'nem, that's the pa-leece. We got too many pales in this bitch. I'm finna do the race."

Big Worm's eyes got big, and for a fleeting moment he was frozen in place, as if the police were behind him and not behind a completely different vehicle miles away. He ended the call in a hurry and turned to Bam.

"Twelve just got behind Pee Wee n'em," he said, the words spilling out of him in a rush. "He about to do the race."

"That's a Hellcat," Bam replied with a shrug. "He'll get away."

Big Worm ran his hand down his face. He was on edge, his nerves becoming more and more frayed by the hour. He popped two more roxies and chased them down with a swallow of Bam's cold narcotic beverage. He flexed his left hand, almost hoping for a throb of pain. But none came. Roxycodone was a miracle drug.

Bam lowered his window and blew a stream of smoke out of it. He cranked up the volume on Lil Durk's "Ahhh Ha" and shook the ice in his double cup. Worm shot his eyes, took a deep breath, and zoned out to the drill anthem:

'We been slidin' through they blocks and they don't know we have / Buddy ass got shot and we ain't claim it but I can show his ass / Niggas actin' like they really like that since my brodie died / Just got out the feds, you bring up murders witcho police ass / I told Von to leave that bitch alone, she post on OnlyFans / Catch 'em at apartments they be in 'cause that's our only chance / They don't be outside like you think, they ass be on the 'Gram / Old opps fuckin' wit my new opps, oh man—'

Bam reignited the conversation by suggesting Worm make another call to Bunny.

"She might know somethin'," Bam said. "I mean, if the bitch who beat her up was Whitney, maybe they talked or argued before the fight. She might've heard something from Whitney that'll help us find the money."

"Man," Worm said without opening his eyes, "I done called Bunny like eight times. She ain't pickin' up."

"Then call her again, nigga. We ain't got nothin' but time. Call that bitch eight more times if that's what it takes. You better act like you want that bread back. That's five *million*. We both know niggas that'll kill whole families over that kinda money."

Big Worm exhaled and opened his eyes. In the forty seconds or so since he'd closed them, the rain had come to a complete stop, and the storm clouds were moving on. Was that a sign from the heavens that things were going to work in his favor? He certainly hoped so.

He picked up his phone and dialed Bunny's number again.

Chapter Thirteen

Too wired from the shooting to sit still, Markio set to work finishing what Whitney had started, folding and organizing the clothes from the storage locker and putting them in new trash bags before placing them in the spare bedroom closet where he stashed his duffle bag full of gelato. He kept a few items for himself; fourteen designer belts; and the bucket hats, one a YSL, the other two by Louis Vuitton.

When he finally sat down on the living room sofa and fired up another stick of Newport—his fourth cigarette in the last hour—he found himself again worrying about not having a gun in his possession. In his line of work, guns were a necessity. People robbed drug-dealers all the time. He had promised Big Gabby nearly all of the cash he had on hand, and the $2,500 he'd sent Candace for Whitney's bond had just about emptied his Cash App account. He couldn't afford to get robbed of his last sixteen pounds of gelato.

There was also the possibility that someone close to G-Money might suspect him of being the shooter and come after him. He'd be a dead man if they ran down on him while he was unarmed.

He *Face-Timed* the one person he knew would go nowhere without a gun: Crasher.

"What's up, my boy?" Crasher answered. He was brown-skinned with short dreads and the kind of fat face that guaranteed a loud snore whenever he slept.

"I need you, bruh. Where you at?"

"On my way to you. I told you I was comin' through there."

Markio smiled. He hadn't expected Crasher to make the drive from Minnesota so soon.

"Joe, I need a ChapStick."

A reluctant look came over Crasher's face. "Maaaan," he said.

"Bruh, I swear to Jesus I need you. You know I wouldn't even ask if I didn't. I done kicked some shit off and had to get rid of my pole. It might be up, I don't know, but if it is I don't wanna get caught without it."

After a long moment of hesitation, Crasher exhaled and said, "I'm keepin' my glizzy, but I got a Mac in the trunk. A Mac-10. It takes .45 shells, got a long-ass fifty clip. I'll let it go for a band."

A thousand dollars was a steep price to pay for a compact machine pistol. But Markio needed it—*badly*—so he agreed to the price without a second's hesitation.

"Bet," he said. "Just run me eight racks and the Mac for the two pounds."

"A'ight, I'll be there in about an hour. I'm on the highway now."

Markio sat smoking his cigarette and scrolling through Facebook for the next few minutes. Now it seemed like everybody in Michigan City was talking about G-Money's murder. A boy called Flocka who hung out with Lil' Jimmy had posted a cryptic message insinuating he might be responsible for the shooting: '*Jump mah homie and get turnt to a pack,*' he'd posted alongside a gun emoji. And apparently G-Money had gotten into an altercation with a guy named Smitt at a nightclub in Gary a few nights ago, and a lot of people were saying that might have something to do with it. Markio read the gossip without commenting on any of it. He was glad to see that his name hadn't been mentioned as a possible suspect, but the day was still young.

A sudden knock at his front door startled him. He frowned. Squinted. Said, "Yooo. Who is it?"

"It's me, bruh." It was Fat Jerm. "And I brought you some company."

Markio was cautious by nature. He trusted Fat Jerm to a certain extent, but life had taught him not to trust anyone completely. He peeked through a corner of the blinds and saw Fat Jerm standing on the porch with four others.

Anyssa "Nissa" Chavis, her brother Blubby, Mya, and the girl Mya had introduced as her older sister.

Fat Jerm and Nissa were holding brown paper bags from East Side Liquors. The necks of several hard liquor bottles stuck up out of the bags, as well as a stack of red plastic cups, and Blubby had two big dripping bags of ice.

Markio stepped back from the window and stood as still as a mannequin, his mouth wide open. What the fuck was Fat Jerm thinking? Markio had just murdered a man right in front of Blubby, and now Jerm had brought Blubby right to his front door.

"Uh—here I come," Markio yelled, but he didn't move a muscle.

"Negro, I *just* saw you in the window," Mya shouted. "You better open up this goddamn door!"

It was Mya's sweet and sexy voice that put Markio in motion. He went to the door, unlocked it, and pulled it open.

"We brought the party to you, nigga," Fat Jerm said, walking in like he owned the place. The others followed him in, placing their bags on the living room table, and Blubby carried the ice bags to the kitchen.

"What the fuck is all this?" Markio said.

Mya and her sister paid him no mind. They were doing their little happy dance as they pulled half-gallon bottles of Hennessy out of the bags and cracked them open.

"It was them, bruh," Fat Jerm said, pointing at the girls. "You remember Blubby and Nissa's lil' sister Quee-Quee from Lakeland? Well, she works at Olive Garden with Whit-ney's sister, and she overheard them saying where you lived. I bumped into them at the liquor store, and since they were already on the way over here, I let Josh keep my truck and jumped in with them."

"Yup," Mya said, nodding, her whole body seeming to join in on the nod. "We found out where you live, nigga, and we in this bitch."

"Yeah, believe what she said," her older sister added.

Markio laughed out loud. He felt relieved. He felt happy that a bad bitch like Mya was in his living room, getting ready to turn up. He felt happy that Fat Jerm and Blubby, two of his closest friends, were here with him—never mind what he'd done to one of Blubby's fellow Gangster Disciples a little over an hour ago.

And most of all, Markio felt like drinking.

Mya handed him the first cup she poured. "Drink up," she said, biting her bottom lip and smiling at him.

Markio accepted the cup, grinning and shaking his head at Mya as he watched her fill a cup for herself. He took a big gulp of the cognac that made his entire face scrunch together as the fiery liquid dropped down his throat.

Within minutes the mood was set. Mya's sister—who re-minded Markio that her name was Star—used the 70-inch smart TV to log into her YouTube account, and her playlist of rap music videos began with the throbbing tunes of Cardi B and Megan Thee Stallion's classic "WAP" track. Nissa and Mya rolled three blunts of the gelato Mya had bought from Markio earlier, and everyone but Markio smoked; he was on parole and couldn't risk a failed drug test. He did drink, though, sipping from his cup while Blubby and Fat Jerm snorted cocaine off their pinky fingernails.

Markio didn't drink too much. He drank about half of his cup and set it down on the table. The murder was still fresh in his mind. He knew he had to stay focused, just in case one of G-Money's boys happened to pull up. A nice buzz was all he needed.

He sat on the arm of the love seat and listened as Mya and Star talked about their experience at a local hair salon the previous day. Apparently, the service they'd received wasn't up to the standards they'd grown accustomed to in Chicago. Star wore a tight blue designer dress and heels, and her hair was done in a flawless blond bob like her sister's, but what Markio was most interested in looking at was the diamond Cuban-link necklace she had on, and the diamond encrusted pendant attached to it that spelled out her name.

"You know G-Money got his head knocked off, right?" Nissa said, looking straight at Markio.

His gaze immediately left Star's flashy necklace. His eyes got big. His lips fell apart. It seemed like everyone had turned to look at him when Nissa asked him the question.

"Yeah, I saw it on Facebook," he said, slowly and haltingly.

"Blubby saw the whole thing," Nissa went on. "He said some lil' nigga ran up outta nowhere and blew his brains out. He stood over him for a second too, like, makin' sure he was dead. That's how Blubby and D-Nut seen him, 'cause everybody was walkin' from behind the house when it happened, and G-Money was in the back, so nobody saw the shooter until G-Money was already shot."

Standing next to the sofa where his sister was seated, Blubby regarded Markio with an uncertain smirk, but he kept quiet, and snorted another small mound of white dust off his pinky nail. His dreads were in the beginning stages of growth. He'd been having health problems too, just like Big Gabby;

only instead of losing weight, he was gaining it. He'd ballooned to over two hundred and sixty pounds. He looked bloated. His face was wider, rounder. His hands were as plump as latex gloves with air blown in them. He looked even heavier than Jerm.

"They say who did it yet?" Markio asked, trying his best to sound genuine.

"Flocka basically confessed to the shit," said Jerm. He was eating a Rally's spicy chicken sandwich, a dollop of mayo clinging to the corner of his mouth. "I ain't gon' lie, I thought it might've been you at first. When they said he had beat up on Lil' Jimmy before he got whacked, I automatically thought of you. Everybody knows how much you love Whitney and her kids. But then the nigga Flocka posted some shit on Facebook that pretty much let everybody know he did it or had some'n to do with it. Dumb ass. They probably already got a warrant out for his stupid ass."

"Who is Flocka?" Nissa asked.

Whenever Blubby started stuttering while he was standing, he had a peculiar way of repeatedly stomping his right foot until he got the word out. The right foot began to rise and fall now, as if he were attempting to start up an old moped.

"But ... But, man ... but, m-man, Flocka the lil' nigga who moved up here from Ev ... from Evansville. The lil' ni-nigga who be with Lil J' ... Lil' Jimmy."

"Oh." Markio moved his head back and forth. He'd been seeing the tall brown-skinned teen a lot over the past few months. He was always riding around with Jimmy in Jimmy's yellow Camaro convertible, or playing *Black Ops: Modern Warfare 2* with Jimmy in Jimmy's bedroom. Lil' Jimmy had introduced him to Markio as Aaron, not Flocka.

"Yeah, he's done for," Nissa concluded. "Wherever the hell he is. They gon' have him in cuffs and chains for the next fifteen years like they did you, Markio. He just don't know it yet."

Markio grinned contentedly.

More conversation ensued. In the midst of it all, Fat Jerm pulled Markio aside for a one-on-one talk. He had downed an entire cup of cognac, and Markio could tell that he was more than a little tipsy.

They left the living room for Markio's bedroom. Fat Jerm leaned back against the dresser. Markio sat at the foot of his huge bed, looking down at his phone to read the text he had just gotten from a Southgate resident called Loochie who wanted to cop a half pound.

"What's the word, bruh?" Markio asked, glancing up from his phone.

"Man." Jerm sighed. "Shit. I don't even know how to tell you this shit, bruh, but I ain't gon' feel right unless I tell you. It ain't nothin' really. I just don't like keepin' it from you. I know if the shoe was on the other foot you wouldn't keep it from me."

Markio's head tilted a little to the side. His brow came together in a wrinkle.

"Listen," Jerm said. "A few years ago, when Whitney was fuckin' around with Veezo, I was fuckin' her too. That's why she ended up killin' Veezo. He walked in on us in the bed together, and he tried to choke her out. I had my pants down, and I was tryin' to pull 'em up when he started chokin' her. I would've snatched the nigga up, you feel me, I'd have choked him, but my fuckin' pants were down around my ankles. But she didn't need my help. She grabbed the strap off his hip and shot him."

Markio stared blankly at Fat Jerm for several seconds. Part of him hoped—no, not hoped, *wished, prayed*—that Jerm would burst out laughing and say he was only joking, that he and Whitney had never been intimate. But no laughter came. No chuckle. Not even a hint of a smile. Fat Jerm only stared back, waiting on Markio's response to this heart-shattering revelation.

It took a couple more seconds for the heavy truth of it to fully register in Markio's brain. Then the anger set in. He clenched his teeth and tossed his phone aside. All he could think about was all the weeks and months Whitney had been by his side since he got out of prison last year, and not once had she mentioned that she'd had a sexual relationship with Fat Jerm. Not only that, but she'd also lied to him about what *really* happened the night she killed Veezo. He had just smoked Veezo's closest homie, who had every right to be upset. Whitney had deceived the man she claimed to love, and today he'd put his freedom in jeopardy by killing a man for laying hands on her son.

"My bad, bruh," Jerm said, rubbing his fat hands on top of his bald head. "This one on me. You know you been my lil' nigga ever since you first moved out here from the Chi. I just didn't think you and Whitney were gon' get serious. Now that I see where it's goin', I'll feel fucked up not tellin' you what it was."

"It's cool." Markio waved it off, standing up. "I ain't mad at you. I'll never get mad at my nigga over no bitch. Plus, you know, it ain't like me and you been hangin' out every day like we used to. She the guilty one. That bitch be with me every day. I done told her a thousand times how much love I got for you, and she ain't said shit."

Markio reached out and shook Fat Jerm's hand, not with a regular handshake but with the gang handshake that TVLs and 4CHs had used for decades to symbolize their "Double Solid" alliance. It was much deeper than a regular handshake. There were written laws and principles that came with being a real gang member. Markio had been abiding by those laws for as far back as he could remember.

Mya walked into the room just as they finished their handshake. Her presence instantly lightened the mood. There was a heavy, suffocating ache in the center of Markio's chest, but Mya's sexy smile made him feel a lot better.

"Can me and you talk for a minute?" she asked. "Alone, I mean."

Fat Jerm smiled. Threw up his hands and walked around Mya, leaving the room and pulling the door shut behind him.

Markio picked up his phone and sat back down.

"So," Mya asked, standing at the dresser mirror with her legs scissored and her hands on her hips, "you live here by yourself?"

"Yup."

"What do you do for work?"

"I work from home," he said with a dry chuckle.

"How many kids you got?"

"*None*. Ain't got no bitch either."

Markio heard the spite in his tone of voice and didn't regret it one bit. He tapped into the Facebook app on his iPhone's home screen and blocked Whitney from his page. Then he doubled down and deactivated the page altogether. There were too many photos of him with Whitney on his page, and he didn't want to look at any of them.

"Well, why did you have somebody listed as 'Wifey' in your phone? And don't lie, because I already know who she is. Nissa showed me her Instagram page. It's some bitch named Whitney. She sells lip gloss."

"Maaan, she for the streets. I'm single."

Markio was texting Loochie back, confirming that he had the half pound for $2,500 and that he would front Loochie another half-pound and let him owe an additional $2,500. He went to his Instagram page and briefly considered going through his pics and videos and deleting all the ones with Whitney in them. It was a petty thought, but he was in a petty mood.

He looked up when Mya spun around to face him. She caught sight of the eight steel suitcases standing in two rows of four next to the bed. Her eyebrow rose questioningly.

"Why do you have so many suitcases?"

"I use 'em to hide the body parts of the people who ask me too many goddamn questions."

Mya rolled her eyes, shook her head, and began rummaging through her purse. "I did some research on you," she said, stepping closer to him. "Nissa introduced me to Mae Mae, your ex side boo, and she told me about that dick."

Excitement flashed in Markio's eyes. When Mya's hand came out of her purse holding a box of extra-large Magnum condoms, his mouth spread open in a smile that showed a lot of teeth.

"Mae Mae said I'd need these," she said. Then the pitch of her sexy voice went up a couple of notes. "Is it really that big?"

It was growing bigger by the second. Mya nibbled at her bottom lip and stared wantonly at the print of his dick in his gym shorts as it became thicker and longer with every beat of his heart. She moved forward and climbed onto his lap, planting her knees on either side of his waist. Markio put his hands on her ass and squeezed, pulling her down onto his growing erection. He kissed her on the chin, then on the side of her neck.

"Let me see the rest of that mermaid tattoo," he said, really meaning it.

Mya leaned back a little, laying her bag down next to Markio and peeling the shirt up over her head, and Markio's eyes went as wide as his teeth-baring smile as he took in the tantalizing view of her naked breasts. Her tattoo ended just below the perky globes of flesh. It depicted the mermaid swimming toward a jagged opening in the middle of Mya's chest that showed her heart as an open bank vault piled high with stacks of hundred dollar bills. There were other mermaids coming and going, some dumping their cash-filled bags into the vault, others swimming back toward the jagged opening with their bags emptied.

"And no," Mya said, running her fingertips over the waves in Markio's hair, "that does not mean I'm a gold digger. I just love getting money."

Her explanation was unnecessary. Markio cupped the underside of her right breast in his left hand, and sucked the nipple into his mouth. The cognac in his system had done something magical to his memory: he'd completely forgotten about Whitney, at least for the moment.

"Lock the door first," Mya said.

"Ain't nobody gon' come in here." He went to the other breast and suckled. They were perfect C-cups, nice handfuls of softness.

Mya moved back, pulling herself from his grasp, and planted her Gucci ankle boots on the floor. Markio ogled her fat ass as she walked to the door and locked it. When she turned back to him, he had his dick out. She grabbed her hips and smiled at him.

"Wow," she said.

"What?"

"It *is* really that big."

Markio laughed. Mya might have still been standing by the door, but her perfumed scent was all around Markio, lingering.

"Please tell me you eat pussy," she said, walking to him,

each step slow and deliberate. When he nodded a *yes*, she added, "Don't worry, I ain't fucked nobody since I broke up with my nigga in May. That's on my daddy's grave. And I took a bath before I left the house, just like I do every morning."

"Shut the fuck up and get over here." Markio stood and picked Mya up by the waist. He tossed her onto the bed, grinning as she yelped and laughed. "Take them shorts off."

She kicked off her ankle boots, then peeled off the shorts and threw them aside. They landed on one of the suitcases. In the living room, as a GloRilla song began blaring from the TV, Markio heard Star scream out a ratchet "Aayyy!" of excitement as he climbed onto the bed with Mya.

He pushed her thick legs apart and took a few seconds to admire her pretty pussy before he pinched back the hood over her clitoris and began licking it, plunging a middle finger into her pussy as he did it. She was warm and wet on the inside, much wetter than he'd expected; so much wetter than any pussy he'd ever experienced.

"Ooouuu," she purred, grabbing fistfuls of the fur Louis Vuitton blanket beneath her and throwing her head back in ecstasy. "Ooouuu, Jesus. That's it right there. Just keep doin' that."

Markio progressed from just licking her clitoris to both licking and sucking on it, using his middle and ring fingers to penetrate and loosen up her tight opening, curling his fingers upward so that his fingertips would brush up against her G-spot. The flawless technique sent her body into tremulous spasms. The pleasant scent of her pussy, combined with the glistening juices trickling down off his thrusting fingers, made his dick even harder. He briefly moved lower to run his tongue between her slippery pink vaginal lips before returning his attention to her engorged clitoris.

110

"Damn, you taste so good," he said.

Mya replied with a falsetto of impossibly soft moans, so Markio kept at it, sucking on her clitoris, fingering her pussy, and slurping up her sweet juices until she tensed and let out a high-pitched screech. She pushed down on the top of his head, trembling through a body-seizing orgasm, trying to get his steadily slurping mouth off her clitoris as it became more and more sensitive. But he grabbed her thighs and kept sucking and licking, smiling around the clitoris in his mouth as Mya bucked and shivered.

When her orgasm finally subsided, Markio got up on his knees, biting his bottom lip and staring down at Mya as she tried to catch her breath. He reached for the box of Magnum condoms, took out one of the gold condom packets, and tore open the wrapper with his teeth.

"Wait a second," Mya said, holding up a hand. "I'm sorry. I need a minute. It's been a while." She snickered and blew out a breath of air through pursed lips. "*Shit*! That felt good."

Markio shook his head, ignoring Mya's request to delay the inevitable. His dick was so hard it hurt. He rolled the condom onto his humongous, lengthy erection and eased the head in between her puffy vaginal lips. Her mouth fell open, and she gasped in a great breath as he sank in deep.

King Rio

Chapter Fourteen

Whitney hated the way the rough fabric of the green-and-white-striped Laporte County jail uniform felt against her skin. She hated the racist sheriff's deputies even more. It was crazy that the city of Laporte, where the county jail was located, was just a few minutes' drive from Michigan City. The blatant disdain the deputies showed to black inmates made Whitney feel like she was somewhere far away from home.

She was sitting on the cold steel seat at the desk in the small holding cell they'd put her in an hour ago, her head down and resting on her crossed forearms as she waited impatiently for Candace to come and get her. Her cellmate, a younger black girl named Dejane Robinson, who sometimes hung out with Ava and Eva, sat on the top bunk, her legs swinging merrily over the bedside as she told Whitney about the case that had landed her here in jail.

"I got caught with a pound of meth," Dejane was saying. "That nigga Santana had me drive all the way out to Iowa to pick it up, and I didn't know the whole shit was being watched by the fuckin' drug task force. They pulled me over as soon as I made it back into the city. I ain't gon' lie, I told on that nigga. They still arrested me but the cap said I could get out of it with a lesser charge if I wear a wire on Santana. He called it a "controlled buy" or something like that."

Whitney couldn't believe her ears. She raised her head to look at Dejane. "Girl, listen: Santana is a Black Disciple from Chicago. You know that, right? You know they'll do some'n to you for tellin' on that man."

"So what! It can't be worse than doin' twenty or thirty years in prison. I ain't no street bitch. I just graduated high school last year. And I just found out I'm six weeks pregnant. Fuck that. I'm snitchin'."

Whitney didn't condone snitching. She hated snitches like she hated racist sheriff's deputies. But she laughed at the audacity of the teenager's rash decision. Then she got up and went to the steel intercom box near the door and pressed the button.

Seconds later, a sheriff's deputy beeped in on the speaker: "Yeah?"

"I'm, uhh, waiting to get bonded out. My sister should've been here by now. Can you tell me what's going on?"

"Yeah. Are you Clarrett?"

"Yes. Whitney Clarrett."

"Okay, I think I know what's going on here but wait a sec," the deputy said, and it was almost thirty seconds before he beeped back in. "Okay, yeah. So your family's here to get you, but we're bringing in a few guys who apparently tried fleeing our officers, and for some reason one of our deputies has your sister helping him with an incident report, so it's gonna be a sec."

"Huh?" A confused expression came over Whitney's face. She moved closer to the intercom. "Did you say my sister is helping with an incident report?"

"Yeah. From what I was just told, the four guys we arrested were following your sister while she was on the way here, so she dialed nine-one-one, and when our deputies arrived, the guys tried speeding off, but we got them boxed in. They're walking the guys in now. Someone'll probably be to get you in the next twenty minutes or so."

"Okay. Thank you."

Whitney backed away from the intercom with more questions than she'd had when she approached it. Someone *else* had followed Candace from the hospital? A car full of men? And Candace was filing a report about it? In between these questions Whitney kept thinking what the driver of the Range Rover had told her.

'It's the storage locker. I'm getting fifty thousand for finding out who bought the locker.'

Whitney fell back against the off-white cinderblock wall, looking down at her neon orange jail sandals. She struggled to imagine what might be hidden inside the suitcases. There was obviously *something* in them. Why else would someone pay $50,000 to locate the person who'd purchased the locker? The clothes were worth more than that, for sure, but if someone had enough money to buy the clothes, they had to have a lot more money to blow. So why put such a high bounty on the locker?

"So, your sister must have herself a stalker," Dejane said. "I got one, too. Crazy thing is, it's my boyfriend. I been duckin' his dumb ass 'cause he thinks I'm pregnant by him when I'm really pregnant by his daddy."

Whitney tuned the girl out. She turned and went to the square window in the dark green steel door. Looking out the window, she watched a team of policemen escort four young black men in handcuffs into the jail and sit them on the bench that ran along the low wall across from the booking area. The four boys had dreadlocks, and there was something about them that said: *Chicago*. Maybe it was their dreads, or the slang they used as they spoke with each other, words like "twelve" and "fo'nem" and "joe."

The four young men had their photos taken and were fingerprinted, and a few minutes later they were led past Whitney's door to the group shower area where Whitney had been strip-searched and given her jail scrubs. She remained at the door until they reappeared, and the door to the holding cell directly next to Whitney's popped open. The guard ordered two of them into the cell.

"Ooh! We're getting neighbors!" Dejane said excitedly. "I hope it's some more boys. We can talk to them through the vent."

Whitney turned to look at her, and Dejane pointed at an air vent on the wall just beside the stainless steel toilet. Whitney could already hear the two young men talking, even without being up close to the vent, but she got down on her hands and knees and moved in closer anyway, not wanting to miss a word.

"Ask them their names!" said Dejane.

Whitney gave her cute young cellmate a stern look and brought a shushing forefinger up to her lips. Then she put her ear right up against the vent and listened.

***

"Man, this some hoe-ass shit. On fo'nem." Pee Wee sat at the desk and slammed back against the wall. Lil' Mark, a TVL Pee Wee had grown up with in Chicago's North Lawndale neighborhood, sat down on the bottom bunk across from him. "I would've got away if they ain't block us in like that. I ain't know they was in front of us *and* behind us."

"They swooped in outta nowhere, gang." Lil Mark began twisting one of his dreads, staring down at the smooth concrete floor. "They got us jammed up out here in Redneck, Indiana. We ain't never gon' get out."

They'd been busted with two assault rifles—an AR-15 and a Kalashnikov AK-47—and three handguns, as well as a sack of weed and a bottle of fake Percocet. No one had claimed ownership of the weapons and drugs, so they were all being charged for them.

"You know what?" Pee Wee said heatedly. "I'm about to say fuck Worm *and* Bam. On fo'nem grave, if I find them suitcases, I'm keepin' that shit for myself."

"What's s'posed to be in 'em?"

"Baby Lord called and talked to Bam on the way out here, when Worm was sleep. He says Bam said it's like five million. On fo'nem grave. And I'm not about to just hand over no five million dollars and let them niggas pay us ten racks apiece for findin' it. That shit over with. We gon' keep every dollar of that."

Lil' Mark raised his head. He was a slim brown-skinned thirty-year-old who looked much younger than his age. The green stripes on his baggy jail scrubs were stained and faded. There was a questioning look in his eyes. He was trying to discern whether or not Pee Wee was telling the truth about the contents of the suitcases they had traveled here in search of.

"What? You don't believe me?" Pee Wee asked. "Why else would they offer us ten racks apiece to come out here and find some suitcases? That's eighty thousand. And you know Baby Lord don't be cappin' anyway. If he says that's what Bam told him, then that's what Bam told him."

"Damn. Five million." Lil' Mark lowered his head and started twisting another dread, thinking about all the things he could buy with five million dollars.

***

The door behind Whitney popped open. She rose quickly from her hands and knees as the door was pulled open by an older white female guard.

"Whitney Clarrett?"

"Yes, ma'am."

"You're being released. Roll up that mattress and come with me."

It was as if Whitney were in a trance. She rolled the thin green mattress and held it under her arm as she left the cell, not even acknowledging Dejane's shouted goodbye. She changed into her own clothes on autopilot, and before she knew it she was standing in the jail's front lobby area, receiving hugs from three of her children while Candace told her about the black Dodge Challenger that had followed them halfway here to the jail.

"Who got my phone?" she asked.

Candace gave her a look. "Did you hear anything I just said?"

"Yes, I heard you. It's just—I know why they keep following us. That's why I need my phone. I need to call Markio."

"Ava said, "It's in the car, in your purse."

"Okay, let's go. I'll ride with Candace so me and her can talk. Ava, you just follow us. And Joselyn, Jimmy, I don't want either of you on your phones. Y'all need to be lookin' at every car on the road, makin' sure nobody's following us."

Together, the five of them walked out of the county jail and across the parking lot. Candace and Whitney's cars were parked side by side. Whitney got her purse and then joined Candace in the 300C.

"What the hell is going on?" Candace asked, backing out of the parking space. "This is about more than G-Money. I can feel it."

"G-Money ain't got nothin' to do with it." Whitney dialed Markio's number and put it on speaker as the line began to ring. "It's about that storage locker Markio got from the auction this morning. The suitcases. They want what's in the suitcases."

The ringing came to an end and went to Markio's voicemail. Whitney sighed out and typed out a quick, urgent message to Markio: '*CALL ME ASAP!*'

"So, what's *in* the suitcases?" Candace asked.

"Money, I think." Whitney redialed Markio's number, then looked out her window at the side mirror. Her Honda was right up on the Chrysler's rear bumper. As they made a turn, she saw that there was a gray Town Car behind her Honda, then an Audi SUV. Both of them had white people in the driver's seats. "I just overheard two of the boys who followed you here talking about it. One of them said the suitcases are filled with money. They're being paid ten thousand dollars apiece to come out here and find the suitcases. And the girl me and Eva beat up said the same thing. She got paid *fifty* thousand."

"I don't understand. Why come after you? You didn't buy the locker."

"See, that's the thing. I did—on paper, at least. I filled out the paperwork when Markio paid for the locker. I mean, he's my man, you know? I didn't even think about it. And I think that's how they got on me. My address and phone number was on the paper I filled out. My name, too. They must have got somebody to give them that paper."

"And Markio never even opened the suitcases to see what was in them?"

Whitney ended the second call after hearing the voicemail start up again and shook her head. "Nope. He was too busy sellin' weed. I need to get over there and talk to him."

"How much money do you think is in the suitcases?" Candace pressed.

Whitney looked over at her. "You wouldn't believe me if I told you."

"Try me."

***

There were three of them in the silver Chevy Silverado: D-Nut, Leezo, and Polo. They were the others who'd introduced the undersides of their sneakers to Lil' Jimmy's face. Dennis "D-Nut" Carter, a forty-year-old former member of the Fifth Ward Black Disciples who'd flipped to a Gangster Disciple for a kilo of cocaine in 2008, had the coldest heart of the three. He had murdered five men in his past, and today he was going to score again. He had a Heckler & Koch MP5 submachine gun wedged in between his seat and the center console, a 32-round banana clip curving out from under it.

In the driver's seat, driving with one elbow on the ledge of the open window and the other hand on the steering wheel, was Bartholomew "Leezo" Thompson, twenty-eight years old, a chubby dark-skinned Gangster Disciple from 63rd and St. Lawrence on Chicago's south side, better known as Tookville, named after Shondale "Tooka" Gregory, a DG who'd been murdered more than a decade ago. Leezo hated drill rappers Chief Keef and Lil' Durk more than he hated anyone on earth, because for years they'd put thousands of dollars on the heads of his fellow gang members, getting their brains blown out before they had the opportunity to make anything of themselves. Leezo had slid on the "O-Block" and "Lamron" Black Disciples, collectively known as the 300 Black Disciples, day and night for years, speeding down Normal and King Drive and Eggleston, jumping out, chasing after and gunning down several BDs in retaliation for his dead homies. He'd moved away after learning that someone had put $100,000 on his head. He'd only been in Michigan City for about eight months. He'd known G-Money from Menard, when he was serving time for an attempted murder, and he'd met D-Nut in Cook County Jail's infamously ruthless *Division 9* a few years before that, so when he heard they were in Michigan City, he'd linked up with them immediately.

In the back seat, sitting with an AR-15 with a 120-round drum and a bump stock that made the assault rifle spit rapid fire stretched across his narrow lap, was Jermaine "Polo" McCoy, the only one of the three GDs who was actually from Michigan City. His half-sister was Janet McCoy, G-Money's girlfriend, with whom G-Money shared three young children.

They were driving from neighborhood to neighborhood, in search of the bone-white Mercedes Benz truck they knew belonged to Markio Earl.

No one had seen Markio's truck fleeing the scene of the murder. D-Nut was going off speculation. G-Money had been killed right after receiving a warning from Blubby that Markio was Whitney Clarrett's boyfriend, and that Markio was dangerous. Flocka's threatening post on Facebook had everyone thinking he had killed G-Money but D-Nut knew Flocka couldn't be the shooter because Flocka was over six feet tall and the masked gunman who shot G-Money was short, like Markio. D-Nut and Blubby had seen the shooter. D-Nut's gun had been in the Chevy pickup, and by the time he retrieved it the shooter had vanished.

"Don't he sell loud or some'n?" Leezo asked as he crept through the Normandy Village apartment complex, looking for Markio's truck.

"Yeah, he got that gelato on deck," D-Nut said. "I don't know his number. I buy my weed from the folks, either from Loochie or Reggie. I ain't shoppin' wit' no Vice Lord."

"I got him on Facebook," said Polo. "Hold on, let me find his page." Ten seconds later he said, "Damn, he must've deactivated his page. I just had him on here yesterday. He posted about a crib he just got."

"You know what the crib looks like?" D-Nut asked.

Polo shrugged. "He only said it's a house. Didn't post no pics or nothin'."

"Maaan." Leezo shook his dreads and reached for the rearview mirror, positioning it to look back at Polo. "You mean to tell me we been lookin' through all these apartment complexes for this nigga, and the whole time you knew he lived in a house?"

"Yeah, but he sells weed," Polo reasoned. "He could be anywhere."

D-Nut waved it off. "Just drive, G. Slide past Comb Street again. See if his truck is over there." He put fire to the end of a Newports ciggie and stared ahead, his mind set on finding Markio and putting him in the dirt.

Chapter Fifteen

Mya had turned over and put her head down on the silk Louis Vuitton pillow case, her ass raised in the air, her knees spread a foot apart.

Markio thought it was a wonderful view.

He was watching her creamy juices accumulate along the length of his rubber-sheathed dick as he slid it in and out of her virgin-tight pussy. Her booty jiggled with his every thrust, and he loved the sight of it. He ran the palms of his hands over her ass and lower back as he fucked her, her euphonious moans encouraging him to drive in deeper and deeper. Mya put one hand between her thighs and fiddled with her clitoris. The fingers of her other hand were splayed out on the headboard.

"I'm about to come again!" She said it twice, and then her words came to fruition as she threw back her head and let out an opera-like high note of sexual release.

Markio held on and kept hammering in and out of her for several more seconds. Then he dug in deep and held his convulsing erection inside of her as he ejaculated. It was an intense orgasm that lasted a while. Markio's dick jerked and twitched sporadically as he spilled his seed, and when he finally pulled out he was shocked to see that only the ring of the condom covered the base of his dick.

The condom had broken.

"Oh, shit," he said.

"I know. Fuck. That felt as fuckin' good." Mya rolled over and lay flat on her back, her head sunken into the goose-down pillow, her chest rising and falling. She closed her eyes and waited for her breathing to normalize.

"Nah. That ain't what I mean. Look."

Mya opened her eyes and looked. When she saw that the condom had broken, she gasped, holding her mouth wide open as she sat up for a closer look.

"You nutted in me," she said, fluctuating tones of amazement.

"Well, it damn sure didn't go in the condom."

"Oooh, you slick bitch. You know they overturned Roe v. Wade. The hell is wrong with you? You tryna get me knocked up?"

Markio cracked up laughing. He slipped off the bed, picked up his wife beater and gym shorts, and put them on. He put on his Jordans and picked up his phone from the foot of the bed. He'd seen it ring twice with calls from Whitney, and he hadn't even considered answering the calls.

"I don't know how I was able to take all that dick in my lil' bitty coochie." Mya pulled on her booty shorts. "I better not get pregnant." She climbed off the bed and picked her shirt off the suitcase. "And I better not catch anything. Because if I do, that's your ass, Mr. Postman."

"You tweakin'. I ain't got no diseases." Markio sat on the side of the bed, his legs a mere two feet away from the nearest suitcase. Mya stood in front of him, hands on her hips. He smacked her hard on the thigh, biting his lower lip and smiling around it.

"Ouch!" She rubbed at her thigh, took a step back, and fell over the suitcases behind her. Marko reached out and grabbed her wrist, keeping her from going down with the steel suitcase.

All but one of the suitcases toppled over.

"Damn, my bad," Markio said, closing his arms around her waist and laughing. "I did not mean to do that."

"A'ight, nigga. Don't get fucked up." She shoved his forehead with her fingertips. "Where is the bathroom?"

"Step out there and turn right. It'll be right in front of you."

Mya grabbed her purse and turned toward the door, and Markio gave her another sharp smack, this time on the ass, as she stepped around the toppled suitcases and unlocked the door.

With the loud music playing in the living room, Markio hadn't realized that more house guests had arrived until Mya pulled the door open. He could only see a small section of the living room from his bedroom, and in that small section he saw Big Gabby and her aunt Crystal. He'd texted his address to Gabby so she could come and pick up the money, so he wasn't surprised to see her and her aunt. However, he *was* surprised to see Snotts and Tooter, two Dub Life niggas he looked at like family, walk past in the living room a second later. Then a pretty brown-skinned girl named Makayla walked past.

What the fuck? Markio thought. *How did they even find out where I live?*

Then it came to him: Nissa and her big mouth.

He got up and walked out to the living room. Star and Nissa gave him the look that said they knew exactly what he and Mya had done. There were two others present, Makayla's older sister—Jessica—and Markio's closest friend, Reggie, a coal-black hustler with a mouthful of gold teeth. Reggie wore an all-white Alexander McQueen outfit over matching sneakers. His front pockets were stuffed with cash, and he had a thick blunt burning between the first two fingers of one hand, a double-cup of iced Lean in the other. Everyone else had cups of Hennessy, and there was weed smoke everywhere.

Big Gabby came forward and wrapped her arms around Markio. "Thank you so much," she said, and when she pulled back he saw tears brimming along her lower eyelids. "I cannot thank you enough. You are literally saving my life."

"You know I'll do it a thousand times. I'm about to go grab it now," Markio said, heading back to his bedroom and waving for Reggie to join him.

"Nigga," Reggie said. "Who is that bad bitch out there with Nissa?"

"That's Star, my new lil' bitch sister. They from Chicago too." Markio went around the fallen suitcases to his closet, looking down at their large steel suitcases as he moved. He noticed that one of them—the suitcase that had landed at the very bottom of the pile—had opened a little. Just a crack.

"That's some solid shit you doin' for Gabby. I'll put a lil' some'n wit' it."

"Where you been all week?" Markio asked, grabbing the backpack off the shelf in his closet. "Shit been crackin' out here."

"Just got back from Cali," Reggie said. "Had to re-up, another hun'ed bows of gelato. Let me know when you need another twenty." He put his double-cup down on the dresser and picked up the corner of the fur blanket to test the fabric. "Man, where you get this from? I was gone for three days, and you done bought Louis sheets and blankets?" He laughed and sat down on the bed.

Markio looked at the door to make sure no one was close enough to hear what he said next. When he saw no one, he looked at Reggie and said, "I'm the one who got G-Money out the way. Between me and you."

"You *know* I ain't surprised. I still remember when you shot up 10th Street and Littles called me to come pick y'all up." Reggie chuckled once. "So you back on that, huh?"

"He put his hands on my lil' nigga. You know I can't go for that. I ain't lettin' nobody touch me or nobody I got love for." Markio put the backpack on the bed and began lifting the suitcases back into standing positions. "I need a strap, though."

"What happened to the glizzy?"

Markio gave Reggie a look.

"Aw, okay. A'ight. Well, shit, I got my girl strap on me now, but I got a .45 Ruger in the car. Got a couple more straps at my other bitch crib. Two nines and a forty. Only choppas I got is the Draco and the Norinco Mac-90 I bought from Sway. Which one you want?"

"I just need some'n to go and make this play. My nigga Crasher got a Mac for me, but I don't wanna go and meet up with him without a pistol on me. Especially after what just happened with G-Money. Can't get caught lackin' like they caught Biggs."

Reggie nodded. "I'll go and grab that Ruger for you now." He got up and left the room just as Markio was lifting the last suitcase by its handle.

The suitcase fell open, and out tumbled dozens of rubber-banded bundles of cash.

Markio's mouth dropped open. His eyes bulged. "Aw, *hell* yeah!" he shouted, then remembered he had a house full of guests and chastised himself for the revealing shout.

He snatched his backpack off the bed and rushed to the door with it just as Mya was returning from the bathroom. "Here, hand this to Gabby," he said quickly.

"Hand it to who?"

"Big Gabb. The biggest girl in the living room." Markio thrust the backpack at Mya and shut the door in her face, hastily engaging the lock before he ran back to the open suitcase.

He picked up two of the thick cash bundles—one a pile of fifties, the other a massive stack of hundreds—and fanned through them. There was easily fifty grand in the pile of hundred-dollar bills.

"Who in the fuck would leave this in storage and not pay the bill?" Markio uttered the question aloud to himself, in fluctuating tones of disbelief.

And before he knew it Mya was back at the door.

"Markio?" She tried to turn the doorknob. "Why you lock the door?"

Then Reggie: "Yeah, nigga. The fuck you lock the door for? You knew I was comin' right back in."

"One second, y'all," Markio said, surprising himself with the level of calmness in his voice as he began piling the cash back into the suitcase, his heart drum-rolling in his chest.

Not all of the cash had fallen out of the suitcase, so it didn't take Markio long to refill it. Maybe twenty seconds at the most. He could have finished sooner, but he kept pausing to look at the bundles of cash, and he took at least five seconds shifting a bundle of hundreds into each of his front pockets. It almost felt like a dream. He'd never seen this much case in his life. There were hundreds of thousands of dollars in the one suitcase alone, and as he walked to the door to let in Mya and Reggie, he wondered if the other suitcases were also filled with cash.

If they were, he was *rich*.

Markio opened the door wearing a smile that spanned the entire width of his face. He wrapped Mya in a bear hug and picked her up, swinging her around in a circle before setting her down again. Mya laughed the whole time she was in the air.

"Okay, I know my pussy good and all but you seriously need to calm down," she said.

For a moment Reggie looked amused. He was seeing an entirely different Markio than the one he'd seen a few minutes ago. Markio kissed Mya on the jaw and picked up his phone.

Whitney was calling again. He ignored the call and looked down at the bulging pockets in his gym shorts.

"I need to change clothes right quick," he said, as Reggie handed him a .45-caliber Ruger P90. He gave the gun to Mya. "Put that in your purse."

"I'm about to go pick my bitch up from work," Reggie said. "Hit my line. And watch out for that silver pickup truck D-Nut and Leezo be in. You know they fucked with dude."

Mya frowned, looking at Markio as Reggie walked out. She dropped the bulky pistol in her large Gucci bag and put her hands on her hips, but she didn't say a word. Markio went to his dresser and pulled open a few drawers. He selected a pair of black Amiri jeans and a black-and-white Amiri t-shirt and switched out his gym shoes for the jeans, pulling out the two rubber-banded piles of blue-faced hundreds and stuffing them down into the front pockets of his designer jeans.

Mya shook her head, a growing smile playing at the corners of her sexy mouth.

"Ain't nothin' like seein' a man with his own money," she said. "You're the first person I've seen out here with that kind of money. I can't even lie, it makes me like you even more. The only person I know who walks around with that much money on them is my oldest brother, the one you grew up around on Trumbull."

Pulling the t-shirt on over his wife beater, Markio turned from the mirror and regarded Mya with a questioning stare. "Yeah, you did say that, didn't you? What's his name?"

"Boy, you know my big brother. He the leader of y'all gang over there. They call him Bam. My other brother's name is Worm."

***

"Look! That's the car! That's the car that was following us!"

Whitney looked ahead through the windshield at a blacked-out Dodge Challenger, thinking there was no way the same car that had followed Candace from the hospital could already be back on the streets. The police had to have towed it.

"No, that can't be it."

"I'm telling you, Whitney. That is *it*."

They were stopped at the red light on Vail Street and Michigan Boulevard, getting ready to make the left turn and drive down to Markio's house. The Challenger was in the northbound lane, also stopped by the red light. Whitney could see two young black men in the front seats, one in the passenger seat with long dreads hanging down around his head, the other with short hair.

Whitney slipped a hand into her purse and pulled out her pistol. It was a 9-millimeter Glock 26 with a ten-round magazine. With one round already chambered, she had eleven shots, more than enough ammo to fend off any attacker.

Candace started panicking. "What the fuck, Whitney! Dial nine-one-one. You have to dial nine-one-one. The other boys they arrested had *assault* rifles. You need to tell them that *Markio* has their suitcases, that we don't have anything to do with that."

"Calm down, sis. Just drive. Just make the turn and we'll see if they follow us."

Candace nodded frantically, holding the steering wheel in a death grip.

"Calm down," Whitney repeated, and she realized she was saying it more to calm herself than to calm her sister. "They're not even looking at us."

She spoke too soon. Before the last word could even fall off her tongue, she saw the eyes of the boys in the Challenger settle on her and Candace. The driver raised a smartphone, training the rear camera on the front of Candace's shriek, half a second before the light turned green. "Oh, my God. I'm calling the police."

"No. Just drive."

Candace made the turn. Behind them, Ava made the turn. And behind Ava, two seconds later, the black Dodge Challenger rounded the corner. Whitney saw it in her side view mirror. Her palms became shaky on the pistol she held firm in her hands. Her mind went back to something she heard through the jail vent. Someone had offered the boys ten thousand dollars each to find the suitcases, and that someone had paid eighty grand. Which meant there were four more men looking for the suitcases, and Whitney was willing to bet that all four of them were in the Challenger.

She looked ahead and saw Markio walking out the front door of his house—with his arms around the waist of another woman.

Markio and the woman—a short, thick redbone with blond hair—were approaching a black Mercedes-Benz G-Wagon that was parked right in front of his house. Fat Jerm and two other women were waiting at the G-Wagon, while several others walked toward other vehicles. Whitney spotted Blubby and Tooter, the two of them getting inside Tooter's two-tone blue 80's model Chevy Caprice on enormous gold 30-inch rims. Snotts, and two girls that Whitney couldn't quite see good enough to identify, climbed into his (Snotts') candy gray Yukon Denali, which also squatted over gold 30's.

"Stop the car right here. Just pull over and park," Whitney said.

"Is that Markio right there?" Candace asked as she pulled to the curb across the street and five houses down from Markio's house.

Whitney said nothing. She threw open her door and stepped out, holding the gun down at her side. She watched Ava pull up alongside Candace's car and lower the passenger window. She was almost too hurt to look in Markio's direction, so she focused all her attention on the Challenger idling behind her Honda.

"Ma, why y'all stop here?" Ava shouted.

The passenger door of the Challenger flew open and the boy with the dreads jumped out holding what looked like a miniature AK-47. There was a name for the gun, but Whitney's brain was processing too much information to think of it. The boy holding the mini AK aimed it at Whitney as he ran around the rear-end of the Chrysler.

"Come on over here, bitch. You gettin' in the car with us," he said.

Overwrought with emotion—fear for her family's safety, anger at the man pointing a gun at her chest, and heartache from catching her man with another bitch—Whitney whipped the Glock up from her side and pulled the trigger, hoping the seven or eight visits she'd made to the shooting range in the months following Veezo's death would pay off.

Those sessions turned out to be well worth the few hundred she'd spent on them. She shot the boy right through the nose, and before he hit the door she had her gun aimed at the Challenger, firing into the windshield. She sent three rounds through the glass just above the steering wheel. She heard Candace and Ava scream and saw her Honda speed off down Vail Street.

Super Gremlin

The Challenger's rear tires spun up twin clouds of smoke as the driver stomped on the gas. The car fishtailed and careened from side to side as it rocketed forward. Fearing that they might be going after her children, Whitney fired five more rounds into the Challenger's passenger side, aiming for the backseat passengers. She didn't lower her weapon until the car made a sharp left turn and roared off down a side street. A great feeling of relief swept through her as she watched her Honda screech to a stop in front of Markio's house. She turned back to the boy on the ground and studied his crumpled figure. He'd landed on his back with his head and shoulders hanging over the curb, his dreads splayed out in a growing pond of blood, his Draco— *that* was the name that had eluded Whitney a moment earlier—still cradled against his narrow chest.

Whitney looked east and saw that her kids had abandoned her car in the middle of the street. Three of the Honda's four doors were wide open. Whitney's children were cowering on Markio's front steps, watching their mother with wide, panic-stricken eyes. The G-Wagon was speeding off in reverse. Snotts and Tooter were fleeing the scene as well. Markio had crossed the street and was running down the sidewalk toward Whitney, his right hand clutching a large-caliber handgun.

In a split second before Markio made it to her, Whitney decided not to confront him about what she'd just seen. If it was true that she had five million dollars in those suitcase, the last thing in the world she wanted to do was get into an argument with him and push him away. As far as she was concerned, he owed her. She'd already gone to jail over the suitcases, and now she'd killed a man over them. Plus, she'd signed *her* name on that bill of sale. And it had been her idea to go to the auction in the first place. They were going to split the money 50/50. She didn't give a damn what (or *who*) he did after that.

Markio closed his arms around her, and she fought the urge to shove his back. "Just go," she said. "I got this. And you know you're on parole. Put up that gun and go. We'll talk later."

He nodded, walked backwards a couple of steps as he looked down at the dead gunman, then tucked his pistol and ran back toward his house.

***

Pulling his white Mercedes truck out of the alleyway that ran alongside his home, Markio braked and looked westward. Half a dozen MCPD patrol cars were already on the street, two of them blocking off Vail Street at Michigan Boulevard. Several uniformed officers were out on foot, canvassing the crime scene and talking to neighbors. Whitney and Candace were standing across the street from the dreadhead Whitney had shot in the face, speaking with Martin Swiztek, the lightning-fast white man who'd chased down and arrested Markio twice back in the day. That was almost twenty years ago. Swizz was the chief of police now, and Markio didn't want any problems with his old nemesis, so he turned east and drove the speed limit until the police vehicles shrunk down to nothing in his rearview mirror. Then he turned onto Springland Avenue and increased his speed by a few miles per hour.

He looked in his rearview mirror again and pulled to the side of the road as three MCPD vehicles with their sirens wailing raced past him. He had to rise up off his seat to see over the suitcases piled on the backseat behind him. He'd had Fat Jerm, Blubby, and Tooter help him load the suitcases into the truck, paying them a crisp $100 each for the quick work.

His phone rang as he was pulling back onto the road. It was Mya calling. He answered and smiled as her sexy voice blossomed from his speakers.

"Maaan," she said, really drawing out the word. "What the hell was that? Nissa said that was your girl Whitney shootin' at that car."

"Tell Nissa to stop talkin' so goddamn much. And tell her not to tell nobody else where I stay. I just moved in and she done already told ten people where I live."

"We just dropped her off. What do you want me to do with all this weed you put in my purse?"

Markio had given Mya the two vacuum-sealed pounds of gelato to hold for Crasher, and he'd put the duffle bag holding the other fourteen pounds in the rear storage compartment of his truck. He was thinking ahead, just in case his name came up in G-Money's murder investigation and the police or his parole officer paid him a visit.

He said, "I need you to link up with my nigga Crasher when he gets in town. He should be here any minute. Meet him in the Knights Inn motel parking lot and give the two bows to him. He'll have eight thousand and a pole for me. Grab that and then get us a suite at the Marriott. It's right across the road from that motel."

"Okay, text me his number. I'll go there now. And I'm about to text you my sister's number so you can send it to your friend, the black-ass nigga with the gold teeth. I guess she got a lil' crush on him or whatever."

Markio laughed. "I got her. I'm about to hit him up in a minute."

"Okay. Oh, and my big brothers are here too. My mama just called saying they pulled up about an hour ago. They're at her house now. I would say we can stop by there so you can see them but she said Worm is in one of his moods, all mad about somethin', and I'm not tryin' to go home just to argue. I'm feelin' too damn good right now."

"That's cool. Just handle that business for me. I'll meet you at the Marriott in thirty minutes."

Mya said okay and ended the call, and Markio thought about the decades-long friendship he'd had with her brothers as he drove to his own mother's home. Worm and Bam were older than Markio by four or five years. Worm had never really been involved in any real gang activity, at least not back when Markio spent all his summer days and nights on the west side of Chicago, but Bam had always been an outstanding member, never hesitating to get his own handles bloody for the gang. Which was why Bam had been made a 5-Star Universal Elite for the Traveling Vice Lords, one of the highest ranks attainable.

Big Worm was a 3-Star Universal Elite, and that was only because of his brother's status in the mob. That and the fact that Worm had paid well over a million dollars in dues to the gang. Financing everything from drugs and advanced weaponry to criminal defense attorneys for the dozens of younger gang members who put in work on the streets. Markio had heard all about the shooting that nearly killed Worm back in April. Lil' Bill, one of Markio's four older brothers, was currently dating Poochie, the woman whose house Worm was parked across from when he was shot. Lil' Bill had called Markio immediately after the shooting and told him Worm was dead, and people had made R.I.P. posts about Worm for almost twenty-four hours before Bam made a post saying Worm had actually survived the shooting.

A silver pickup truck appeared in Markio's rearview mirror and snatched his mind away from the memories of Mya's brothers. He pulled the Ruger from under his shirt in a flash, only to realize a second later that it was a Ford F-150 and not the Chevy Silverado he knew belonged to Leezo.

He paused at a stop sign and sent Crasher's phone number to Mya, his eyes constantly darting around to check his surroundings. Then, he FaceTime-called Reggie, who answered on the fourth ring.

"Bruh, I need you," Markio said before Reggie could even say what's up. "I'm out here lookin' all in the rearview mirror, paranoid and shit. Got this blick on my lap when it's a hundred police out here. I need another pair of eyes. Shit, you know Leezo n'em better than I do. You already know what I'm on."

"I was on my way to you anyway," Reggie said. "Where you at right now?"

"On my way to my mama crib. Just meet me at the Marriott in thirty minutes. And bring that Mac-90 with you. I'm steppin' on G-Money whole clique. One of 'em just hopped out on Whitney with a Draco." Markio chuckled once. "She slumped his stupid ass."

"Damn, that was her? I just heard about that shit. That's two murders in one day. It's gon' be hot out here, bruh. You at least gotta lay low until later tonight."

"I know. That's why I'm gettin' a suite at the Marriott. Just grab us some KFC and meet me there. And get enough food for four people. My new lil' bitch and her sister gon' be there."

"The one who had on that tight ass blue dress?" Reggie asked, and Markio didn't have to look at the phone screen to know that Reggie's gold teeth were on full display.

"Yeah, that's who it is. She just had her sister shoot her number to me so I can give it to you. Bring some blunts and a couple percs, too. For me."

"Thought you wasn't tryna fail no piss test?"

"Man, fuck that shit. Like Durkio said, tell my P.O. I'm high as Duck. I'm back on what I used to be on."

It was true. A switch had flipped in Markio's head. He drove differently, speeding from block to block, sitting at the edge of his seat with his hand on the Ruger. He watched every black male pedestrian he passed on the street, especially the younger men and teens with their hats turned to the right side of their heads. It had been years since the last time Markio was forced into savage mode, and he welcomed the adrenaline rush that came with it.

Markio was under the impression that it was G-Money's folks who'd gone after Whitney. Although he'd planned on breaking it off with Whitney over her history with Fat Jerm, he still loved her, and if G-Money's gang was bold enough to go after his girl then they were certainly bold enough to come after him.

So, as far as Markio was concerned, it was on sight with Leezo, D-Nut, and anyone he caught outside with them.

Chapter Sixteen

Two hours later Markio was sitting on a white leather sofa in his $400-a-night Marriott Hotel suite, smoking a Backwoods cigarillo Reggie had filled with a stronger strain of gelato called Black Cherry that was apparently much more expensive. He had swallowed a 30-milligram Percocet and was sipping from a Styrofoam cup of iced cream soda mixed with four ounces of Actavis Promethazine with Codeine. The combination of drugs had him on another level, but he was focused.

Reggie hadn't brought the Norinco Mac-90, but he had brought a Micro Draco with a 50-round banana clip and two 9-millimeter Glock with steel switches attached to the back of them that turned them into fully-automatic machine pistols. The Mac-10 Mya had gotten from Crasher lay next to Markio, and his hard dick was sliding in and out of Mya's pretty mouth as she kneeled on a pillow between his legs, naked except for the Gucci visor cap she wore turned to the back on her head.

She'd been sucking his dick for about fifteen minutes and he was nowhere near a climax, despite the incredibly great feeling of her sopping wet mouth going up and down his length. She took it out from between her saliva-coated lips and smacked it all over her sexy face.

"Let me hit that shit," she said, reaching for the blunt.

Markio gave it to her and picked up his phone, which also lay next to him, right next to the two huge bundles of Benjamins. He'd taken the rubber bands off one of the bundles, and now the hundreds from that bundle spilled over onto the sofa. He'd counted through them and found that the bundle held exactly $50,000. Reggie and Star had gawked at all the hundreds, and Markio had given the two sisters $1,500 each while they were all eating their KFC meals.

On his iPhone, Markio scrolled aimlessly through his long list of contacts, trying to decide who all would be receiving an unexpected financial blessing. He went to his new text messages and told all his weed customers that he was all out until next week. He *Googled* "2022 Mercedes 5-class" and looked through the results, bookmarking a few of them for later. He went through Johnny Dang's website, looking at jewelry, trying to imagine himself with diamonds on his teeth. He looked at mansions for rent on *Airbnb*.

Then he had an idea.

He went to Nissa's contact info and spent a couple of seconds thinking out his idea. Then he *FaceTimed* her. She picked up immediately, and from the loud music playing in the background he assumed she had found herself another place to party. He could see that she was in someone's house, possibly in a dining room, surrounded by a few younger black men and women. Markio recognized the drill music. It was Wooski, a Gangster Disciple who was one of drill rapper Lil' Durk's biggest rivals.

"Hello?" Nissa yelled at the phone. Her eyes widened when she saw that it was Markio.

"Go to the bathroom right quick. I need to talk to you," Markio said. He quickly moved the camera off his face, aiming it at the ceiling until he saw Nissa enter a small bathroom. Then he put it back on his face and smiled at her.

"Don't—Listen, bro. Do *not* come over here. I'm at this little celebration they're throwing for G-Money at Tandra's house, and all they keep talking about is killing you. They think *you* killed G-Money. I told them it was Flocka, but they still believe it was you. It wasn't you, was it? Please tell me it wasn't you."

"Calm the fuck down," Markio said.

He moved his phone aside to look down at Mya. She had spread his plush white Marriott Hotel bathrobe wide open and was jacking his dick in one hand while she sucked on his balls. The feelings produced from her X-rated ministrations made his eyelids flutter for a second. They had showered together after Reggie and Star got their own room across the hall, and neither of them had bothered to get dressed. There was no need. They were hanging out in the suite until nightfall.

"I'm just so stressed about them threatening," Nissa went on. "You know how much I love you, Markio. You're like another brother to me. I don't even know those niggas. I just came to smoke up their weed."

Though it was beyond difficult to focus on the video call now, Markio forced himself to do it. "Where Tandra stay at?" he asked, shifting a bit as Mya took the head of his dick in her mouth and applied a firm suction while she twisted and stroked his length in both hands.

"I can't tell you that, Markio. If you come over here and something happens to you, I would never be able to forgive myself. These niggas got some big ass guns, Markio. And you know D-Nut from Chicago? His crazy ass is one of 'em. His bald-headed ass is the one who got everybody all hyped up."

"Look at this." Markio moved the camera to the pile of hundred-dollar bills spilling over beside him, then turned it back to his face and smirked. "You see all that?"

"Was them all hundreds?"

He nodded. "And I'll give you five thousand just to stay around D-Nut and his guys until later on tonight. After that, you can just unlock the back door, give me the address, and leave. I'll have Mya bring you the money."

Nissa went silent for a long moment. She looked away from the camera. Someone knocked on the bathroom door, and she told them to hold on a minute. "Shit," she muttered under her breath. "Five *thousand?*"

"Make it ten," Markio said.

"Deal," Nissa quickly replied. "But only because you're my bro and I need the money. I'll keep them here as long as I can. I'll even let this nigga Polo eat my ass again, if that's what it takes."

Mya took a moment to laugh at Nissa's comment. She had put the blunt in an ashtray on the table behind her, and now she reached back and puffed on it, shaking her head.

"A'ight," Markio said. "If they leave out, text me and let me know."

"Okay, I'll text you."

Markio ended the call, and for a while he sat and watched Mya do her thing. She was quite talented at sucking dick. She knew how to work her mouth and hands in perfect unison, and she used a lot of spit.

After some time, Markio stood up and stroked his dick fiercely while she sucked on his balls, and when he felt the nut about to burst out of him he aimed and shot a fountain of semen across her sexy face. It landed like ropes on her lips, her nose, and her cheeks, as white and thick as Elmer's glue. She opened her mouth seconds later and caught the last few squirts on her tongue, looking up at him with one eye slimed shut and smiling her pretty smile.

"Oh, shhhit," he said, and trembled once. "You nasty bitch."

"You like it."

"Hell yeah, I like it." Markio continued stroking his dick, smacking its head on Mya's cum-splattered tongue as she kneeled before him, caressing her stiff nipples with both hands and trying with little success to open her glued-shut eye.

It was an image Markio would never forget.

With all the cash he now had in his possession, Markio felt like he had the world in his hands. He had enough money to buy a house, or a couple of houses, if that's what he wanted to do. He could start a business without any worry about the investment. He could finally fall back from the drug game and type up all the urban fiction novels he'd written in prison. He had used a hammer and a flathead screwdriver to crack open two more suitcases after he carried all eight of them into the bedroom he had at his mother's place, and he'd only found more rubber-banded bundles of cash. If all of the suitcases were packed full of cash bundles, Markio figured he had at least two or three million dollars. That was more than enough cash to live comfortably, with all the things he'd ever wanted in life. All he needed now was a bad bitch to share it with. Though he knew he'd always love Whitney, he didn't think he could ever get over her hiding that she'd fucked Fat Jerm. But he liked Mya. He liked her a lot.

And as he watched her get up and stumble off toward the bathroom, her big round ass bouncing freely as she went, Markio thought she just might be the one.

He shook away the thoughts, using the inside of the robe to wipe his dick dry. Now was no time to be thinking of romance. Now was the time to be thinking of warfare. Nissa had just confirmed what he'd suspected all along. G-Money's gang wanted him dead. It had been a long while since he'd had a gang of opps to go after, and with all the cash he had at his disposal, Markio was more war-ready than ever.

Taking another swallow from his Styrofoam cup, Markio picked up his iPhone. He had one more FaceTime call to make.

Chapter Seventeen

It was 6:30 when Bam received a call from Jackboy and E-Dot, the two Vice Lords who'd ridden with Ace and Baby Lord, saying Ace was dead and Baby Lord had been shot in the chest. They had crashed the Challenger after a short police chase, and in an effort to avoid arrest they'd left Baby Lord in the car and got away on foot. E-Dot's pretty boy looks had scored them a ride from some cougar BBW in an Infiniti truck, and they were going to hang out at her place until Bam contacted them later.

By 7:00, Worm's baby mama—Latazia—had arrived at Jesse Mae's lakefront mansion. Worm was asleep when she made it in, and Bam had immediately sent her to bond out Pee Wee, Lil' Mark, Meno, and Bay Bay. Their bonds were high, but Latazia had proof of income from the four day care centers Worm had assisted her in purchasing, so she had no trouble getting them free. She got the boys two rooms at the Marriott Hotel and Bam gave her $40,500 in cash for all the money she'd spent to bond his young gang members out of jail and pay for their hotel rooms, with an extra $10,000 for her services, and for giving Lil' Mark her own personal handgun.

Afterward, Bam and Latazia stood leaning back against the side of his Cullinan, smoking a blunt and enjoying the darkening glow of dusk as it fell over the sky above.

"Something's wrong," Latazia said. "I feel it in my stomach. Y'all ain't never brought the gang out here to Indiana. What's goin' on?"

Bam put on a fake smile. "Nothin'," he said. Nothin' at all."

The look Latazia gave him showed she wasn't buying it.

Bam gazed vacantly at his smartphone, thinking. He wondered why Bunny had yet to answer her phone for Worm.

Then he thought about the few times she'd linked with him while Worm was in a coma, and how good she'd sucked his dick. Maybe she would pick up her phone for him.

He passed the blunt to Latazia and dialed Bunny's number.

She picked up on the first ring. Her bruised face appeared on the phone screen, and Bam was glad to see she wasn't too beat up. She'd covered her face in makeup, but the bruising on her left cheek was still evident, and there was a Band-Aid behind the bangs hanging down over her forehead. She was wearing a dark pair of Christian Dior sunglasses. Judging from the background, she was on an airplane. No, not just any airplane—a private jet.

"You can tell your brother I'm done fucking with him for good," she said assertively. "I really mean that from the bottom of my heart. I got in the car with him in April and almost got my head blown off. I tried doing him a favor today and got jumped on in a parking lot. I don't ever want to see his face again. He can take that fifty thousand dollars and stick it right up his ass."

"The people who jumped you," Bam said. "Who did it?"

"Whitney *fucking* Clarrett. That's who did it. Her and her daughter. Ol' coward-ass bitches. I would've fucked them up one-on-one."

"Did they say anything? About the suitcases, I mean."

Bunny shook her head. "She thought I was following her for somebody named G-Money. She doesn't even know ..." She trailed off, her mouth hanging open.

"What?" Bam pressed. "She don't know what?" All he could think about was the heroin plug and all the millions he'd make if he could only locate those eight steel suitcases. "Tell me. What is it?"

"When she got handcuffed," Bunny said, "she yelled to one of her other kids and said to tell somebody named Markio to check the suitcases. Yeah, that was the name. Markio! I remember it because that's the name of the boy Worm always said he missed, same boy who moved away from the hood a long time ago."

"Markio." The name blew out of Bam's mouth in a thoughtful whisper. He knew only one man named Markio. And that was Markio Earl.

And the last Bam heard, Markio Earl lived right here in Michigan City, Indiana.

***

D-Nut got Markio's phone number from Danielle, a rail-thin brown woman who was called Slow Folks behind her back because of her Cerebral Palsy.

"I hate that bitch," she'd said. "He killed my baby daddy and only did fifteen years for it. I've been waitin' for somebody to get his bitch ass." The disability made her words slur a little, but D-Nut had understood her well enough.

Now he *FaceTimed* the number and stared coldly at the screen until Markio's face appeared behind a haze of weed smoke.

"What's up?" Markio said coolly.

"Man, you know what's up. Where you at? I'm tryna roll you up."

"Turn me into a pack, huh?" Markio chuckled twice. "I'm wherever you want me to be. We can link up ASAP. I ain't duckin' no smoke."

"I'm sending you my location right now, then. Pop out."

Markio nodded. "Put on a raincoat. Heard it's a storm comin' your way," he said, and ended the call abruptly.

D-Nut looked over at Polo. They were standing on the front porch of Polo's girlfriend, Tandra, waiting on Leezo to finish using the toilet. Leezo had eaten two full bowls of Tandra's four cheese chili, and it had his stomach in knots.

The time was 9:07 p.m. and the sun had just left the horizon. There was a slight breeze flowing through the warm night air. Across the street, a group of seven teenage girls were talking and laughing loudly as they walked toward the corner of 6th and Cedar Street, where a tan-colored Buick Regal on gold rims idled at the curb.

"You heard all that, didn't you?" D-Nut asked, glancing at Polo again.

Polo nodded. Due to the increased police presence, they had laid their guns at their feet. This way they were out of any passing police officer's eyesight but within reach in case Markio happened to ride past.

Now Polo picked up his AR-15. "Let's get off this porch, Folks," he said, looking from one end of the street to the other. "We don't wanna get caught right here if they slide through on us. We can duck off in the alley and wait."

"He was sittin' down in a room somewhere," D-Nut said, lighting his last cig of Newports and tossing the empty pack over the side of the porch. "I just sent our location. Long as this nigga Leezo hurry up we can—"

Out of the corner of his eye, D-Nut saw something dark rise up over the side of the porch railing. *Two* dark somethings.

"Aw shit, G!" Polo said, his eyes widening as two men wearing black ski-masks and black hoodies reached over the porch railing, aiming black handguns with 30-round extended magazines.

Polo tried to raise his AR-15. D-Nut tried to reach down and grab his MP5. But the masked gunmen opened fire, and their guns had little steel switches on the backs of them that made them fire on fully automatic. A rapid spray of hollow-tipped rounds stitched across D-Nut's corpulent body as he bent forward for his weapon, hitting him eighteen times from his hip to the side of his head. Polo managed to squeeze off one shot that cut a hole in the porch's wooden floor. Then a spray of nine rounds rattled his face and made a mess of his skull.

As the teenage girls across the street began to scream, the two masked men ran back to the alley and jumped in an old gray 2002 Monte Carlo with 185,000 miles on the engine. The tires churned up a hundred small racks as they raced off into the night.

King Rio

Chapter Eighteen

Markio wasn't supposed to wear his black-and-white Amiri sneakers until Whitney's birthday party next weekend. As he slipped his feet back into the pricey designer kicks, half-watching Mya as she snoozed on the big king bed, he wondered if Whitney had noticed he was wearing the shoes when he ran up to her after the Vail Street shooting.

He picked up his Mac-10 and his smartphone and went to the bathroom. After shutting the door, he leaned back on the wall and *FaceTimed* the former love of his life.

Whitney answered after a couple of rings. Her eyes were red-rimmed from crying. She was sniffling and looking away from the camera.

"I already know you're mad," she said, not looking at him. "Jerm told me he told you everything. I'm sorry, Markio. There's no excuse for me not telling you. I just didn't want to lose you. I swear on all four of my kids, that's the only reason I never told you."

Markio just stared at her for a long while, feeling his ache return to his heart. The drugs coursing through him made the pain more distant, but it was there all the same. He took his gaze off Whitney to glance at the Rolex on his wrist, the rose gold timepiece that had set her savings back a teeth-clenching amount. There was something in him that wanted to forgive her already.

He hated that part of himself.

"When was the last time y'all fucked?" The question fell out of his mouth, and he instantly regretted asking it. "You know what? Don't even answer that. What happened with the police? What they say?"

She started crying again, but only briefly. She sniffled, then wiped her nose with a wadded ball of tissue. "For the record, the night I shot Jervell was the last time I ever fucked with Jerm. And that's on everything I love." She paused, allowing Markio time to reply, and when he said nothing she continued. "But anyway. I just left the police station not even forty-five minutes ago. They questioned me for hours. The boy I shot didn't have any ID on him, but they found the car crashed somewhere on 10th Street. The driver was still in it. I shot him in the chest. Two other boys got out and ran." She paused again, thinking; then: "And oh yeah, the four boys who got arrested trying to follow Candace from the hospital got bonded out about two hours ago. Swizz called to let me know he was sending a patrol car to watch my house. Not that it matters. Somebody already broke in and searched through every room."

"What did you tell the cops, though?"

"I told them the truth. Well—I kinda left out the suitcases. I didn't mention those. I said it must be because of all the designer clothes you got from the storage locker. I think they want to question you, too." She finally looked at Markio, a glimmer of excitement lighting her eyes. "Did you open the suitcases?"

He nodded. "A couple of em."

"Was it really *five million dollars?*"

Markio's brow came together in a wrinkle, and he tilted his head forward an inch, narrowing his eyes. "Five million? Who told you that?"

"I overheard two of the boys who got arrested for following Candace talking about it through the vent in my cell. They had got put in the holding cell right next to the one I was in. Speaking of which, you might wanna warn your boy Santana that Dejane is about to set him up."

"What else did you hear 'em say?" Markio asked. He would text Santana in a minute. Right now he wanted to know everything Whitney had heard from the two boys.

"That was pretty much it. They said some guys named Bam and Worm paid them ten thousand dollars apiece to come out here and find the suitcases. That's why the boy I shot tried to kidnap me. Oh, and that girl me and Eva beat up? She was getting *fifty* thousand just to find out who bought the locker."

Markio heard the rest of what she said, but his mind sort of went blank at the mention of Mya's older brothers. He opened the bathroom door and looked out at Mya. She was still fast asleep on the bed, a sliver of drool hanging down from the side of her mouth, completely nude beneath her bathrobe.

"You said Bam and Worm, right?" Markio asked, just to be sure, as he stepped back into the bathroom, using the barrel of his Mac-10 to push the door shut.

"Mm-hmm." It was Whitney's turn to do the squinting. "So," she said, "you never answered my question. Are the suitcases full of money or not?"

"It ain't five million. I can tell you that now," Markio said, though he believed it very well could be five million dollars. "I ain't counted it out yet, but I think it might be around seven or eight hundred thousand. You know I gotchoo."

Whitney stared silently at him, the somberness in her eyes turning into something else, something harsher, colder.

"I want half," she said finally. "With all the shit I've been through today, I deserve it."

"Let me see how much it is first. I don't know about half, but I'll definitely look out for you and the kids."

She sucked her teeth, and the corner of her top lip rose in a snarl. "Who was that lil' short bitch I saw you all hugged up with? The bitch with the black G-Wagon?"

Markio chuckled. "I'll call you back," he said, and hung up.

He went back out to the sofa and was picking up his cash bundles and stuffing them down in the front pockets of his jeans when his phone buzzed with an incoming text alert. He was typing in the password to unlock his phone screen when another text alert came through.

One text message was from Whitney: '*BITCH!*'

The other was from Sway Swanson: "We at the door.'

Markio went to the bedroom area, sat down next to Mya, and shook her awake. She rolled onto her back, wiping the slobber from the side of her pretty face, and for a couple of seconds Markio just looked at her, not knowing what to say. Did she know about the money? Was she only acting like she was into him to get close to the suitcases?

No, that couldn't be it. It didn't make any sense. She'd seen the suitcases in his bedroom. She could've easily texted someone his location and had them try to run in his house like they'd done at Whitney's place. But she hadn't. Instead, she had given him one of the best blowjobs he'd ever received. Some of the best pussy, too.

"Why are you lookin' at me like that?" she asked.

Markio smiled warily. Shook his head. "Get up. You over here droolin' and shit. Here." He took the Ruger off his hip and laid it next to her. "Go answer the door."

"I didn't hear anybody knock at—"

Someone knocked at the door, cutting Mya off mid-sentence. She smiled and sat up, then grabbed the Ruger pistol and slipped down off the bed, tying her bathrobe shut as she went out to answer the door.

Markio wrestled the untouched bundle of hundreds out of his left hand pocket, and when Shannon and Sway Swanson entered the bedroom behind Mya seconds later, he tossed the huge bundle of cash right at them. Shannon, the darker of the two tall brothers, caught it in one hand, like his NBA Lakers idol—Kobe Bryant.

While Shannon snapped off the rubber bands and started counting the bills, Sway, the brown-hued older brother, walked over to Markio and whispered in his ear.

"We hit up D-Nut *and* Polo. Didn't see Leezo, but we'll catch him later. You got my word."

Markio nodded. "A'ight. That's fifty I just gave Shannon. I'll give y'all ten more when y'all catch up with Leezo."

Sway returned to Shannon's side, and they spent a few minutes counting through all the hundreds. Then they pocketed $25,000 each, and while Mya walked them back out to the door, Markio texted his good friend—Santana—and told him about Dejane's plan to set him up.

When Mya came back, she stood in the doorway with one hand on her hip. Her other hand held the Ruger loosely at her side.

"You're a smart dude, Markio. I'll give you that."

Markio's brow furrowed. His grip tightened around the Mac-10.

"What you mean by that?" he asked.

Mya's sleepy smile widened. She dropped the heavy pistol in her bathrobe pocket, and Markio relaxed a bit.

"I was looking out Nissa's living room window when G-Money got killed," she said, walking toward him. "Did you know that?"

Markio didn't say a word.

"I wanted to see you again," Mya sailed on. "I thought you looked as damn handsome this morning, and I just had to see you one more time. So when I saw your truck, I stood there at the window and waited for you to come out."

She climbed back onto the bed, handed him the Ruger, and stretched out behind him. He began the process of reactivating his Facebook page, nodding a little and listening apprehensively as Mya revealed her secret.

"I was surprised when I heard the gunshot. I almost backed away from the window. You know that's the unwritten rule in Chicago. You hear gunshots, you hit the floor. But I didn't move, and I saw you run up to your truck a few seconds after I heard the gunshot, holding a balled up hoodie in your hands. You jumped in and sped off."

"Who else you tell this to?" Markio asked.

"Nobody. Star and Nissa were in the kitchen baking cookies at the time. They thought it was a firework. I, like, gasped and jumped a little when I heard it, and I was shocked when I saw it was you, but I didn't tell anybody. I *won't* tell anybody. Ever in my life. I swear on my daddy's grave."

Markio nodded appreciatively. Scrolling down his Facebook page, he saw that news of D-Nut and Polo's murders were already the talk of the town. Anyssa Chavis had just posted a status update: '*OMG Y'ALL POLO AND D NUT JUST GOT KILLED ON TANDRA'S FRONT PORCH! THIS SHIT GETTIN' CRAZY!*'

It was Nissa who'd told Markio that D-Nut and Polo were standing out on the porch, and he'd relayed the information to Sway, along with the promise of $20,000 for anyone who killed D-Nut and an extra $20,000 if Polo got taken out with him. So Nissa's seemingly stunned post was really just an attempt at covering her own tracks.

Markio put his iPhone in his now empty left hand pocket and turned to look at Mya. She was propped up on an elbow, watching him with a mesmerized look in her eyes that bordered on obsession.

"This might sound a little crazy to you," she said, "but just knowing that you actually killed somebody made me so fuckin' wet. That's why I pressured Nissa to find out where you lived. I just had to have you. Right after you sped off, I went in Nissa's bathroom and played with my pussy while I thought about you, and I was still horny even after I came all over my fingers. There's just something about a real gangsta nigga that makes me come so hard. You're the first man I've actually been with who I know for a fact is really about that life."

"Yeah?" Markio was tempted to undo the fluffy strings on Mya's bathrobe. It's what the rock-hard length of flesh in his underwear was practically begging him to do. But there was one more matter to address before he would even consider sex with Mya again. "Well, you'll get some more of this gangsta shit later. Get up and get dressed. We got somewhere to go, and only you know how to get there."

"Huh?" She looked confused. "Where?"

"Your mama's house," Markio said, grabbing her shoulder bag and pushing the Mac-10 down inside of it. "I wanna see your brother."

***

Pee Wee and Lil' Mark were standing inside the elevator when the shiny chromium doors separated for Markio and Mya to enter, and it was like a North Lawndale reunion. There were hugs and smiles all around. Not only was Pee Wee's sister Poochie in a committed relationship with Markio's brother Lil' Bill, but many of Markio's childhood years had been spent around Lil' Mark and Pee Wee. Mya had grown up around them too, though Markio hadn't been there to see it.

"What the *fuck* are y'all doin' out here?" Markio asked, laughing.

And before either of them could reply, Star and Reggie walked onto the elevator. Star let out a joyful scream as she too hugged and greeted Lil' Mark and Pee Wee.

"Get the fuck outta here!" Star exclaimed incredulously.

"Man," Pee Wee said, a huge smile glued to his face, "I ain't seen y'all since Cup's funeral, and even that was on a Skype call from my cell at Indiana State Prison."

"Long live Red D," Lil' Mark said, stating their old friend Ressie Cup's other nickname. "You know his son Bankroll Reese the man now. Shorty got a strip club right in the middle of the hood. Wait, I'm trippin'. That's your lil' cousin, ain't it?"

Markio nodded as the elevator doors slid shut. Reesie Cup, who had been a high-ranking TVL and a big-time heroin dealer before he was murdered several years earlier, had fathered two children with Markio's first-cousin Rose Earl. It was Cup who'd first introduced Markio to the heroin game. Markio was just a little boy when he'd stood beside Rose's dining table and watched as Cup and his cousin—Perk— mixed heroin and lactose in a blender and dumped tiny spoonfuls of the powder onto small squares of aluminum.

Lil' Mark's phone began to ring as Star was telling him and Pee Wee that she and Mya had moved to Michigan City's wealthy Long Beach neighborhood with their mother after their father was murdered in 2016. Markio was lifting his own smartphone, intent on snapping a photo of his fellow gang members, when he heard Big Worm's distinctive baritone boom out of Lil' Mark's phone speaker.

"Forget about Whitney. I need y'all to find that nigga Markio. That's who got my suitcases. Call Taquisha and ask her where he stay. Put that pistol on that nigga and make him run that shit if you got to."

For a brief, fleeting moment that seemed like an eternity, everyone looked at Lil' Mark, saying nothing. Mya's jaw dropped. So did Star's. Reggie began to remove the straps of his white leather Alexander McQueen backpack from his shoulders; he had his Micro Draco tucked away inside of it. The two Glocks he'd brought to the hotel with him were now with Shannon and Sway.

Markio reached for the Ruger he'd stuck down in the front of his jeans, but Lil' Mark was faster, whipping out a chrome-plated handgun and aiming it at Markio's face.

"Don't make me do it, bruh," Lil' Mark said. Then, to Worm, he said, "Markio right here on the elevator with us now. He with your sisters and some black-ass nigga with gold teeth."

"He can hear me?" Worm asked.

"Yeah, I hear you loud and clear," Markio said, as Pee Wee hit the emergency stop button, bringing the elevator to an almost immediate halt.

"Good," Worm said, his voice sounding abnormally parched. "I need all eight of those suitcases. You know exactly what I'm talkin' about, too. I just looked through all your pictures on Instagram. You got Whitney Clarrett all over your page, and she said *you* got the suitcases. My bitch heard her yell it to one of her kids in that hospital parking lot, so I know you got 'em. Tell me where they at and I'll let you keep ten thousand. That's the best I can do."

Lil' Mark turned his phone so Markio could see Worm's face, and Markio looked at an older man he had never truly respected. Bam was the real gangsta. Worm was merely a photocopy of his older brother, and he was protected by the gang because of it.

So instead of addressing Worm, Markio looked past the gun barrel and stared Lil' Mark in the eyes. "Bruh, you know me. You already *know* how I get down. Get that pistol out my face, Joe. Or pull the trigger. One or the other."

"Don't make me do that to you, Lord. On Chief James, I'll blow this—"

An ear-ringing burst of gunfire suddenly rocked the elevator. Markio cringed and ducked low, reaching for his Ruger even as he watched Lil' Mark stumble backward with numerous holes appearing across the front of his green Givenchy shirt. Blood began to spread out around the holes as he slid down the wall, but he held on to his chrome pistol and pulled the trigger just as Markio's hand closed around the butt of the Ruger.

The bullet struck Markio in the right thigh and knocked his leg out from under him. He fell sideways, losing his grip on the Ruger before he could even get it out. Lil' Mark lost his grip, too. The chrome gun slipped from his hand and clattered to the floor. Lil' Mark's eyes stretched wide with panic. Breathing shakily, he coughed, and blood sprayed from his mouth.

Markio looked up at Mya and saw that her Gucci shoulder bag had a big smoking hole in its side. Her left hand was buried in the bag, and it didn't take Markio two seconds to figure out what had happened. Mya had fired the Mac-10 through her purse, sending a fully automatic burst of seven .45-caliber rounds through Lil' Mark's designer shirt.

Scrambling to his feet, Markio scooped up Lil' Mark's gun and pointed it at Pee Wee.

"Get the fuck down!" Markio shouted the order, and Pee Wee complied with no hesitation as Markio glanced down at the hole in the right thigh of his jeans.

To his surprise, there was no blood. Just a dime-sized hole right through the middle of the protruding bulge where his bundle of hundred-dollar bills rested in his pocket. He pulled out the cash and gaped at the perfect round hole in Benjamin Franklin's face. The bullet was stuck about a quarter of the way through the stack of cash.

Reggie bent forward and searched Pee Wee's waistline for a weapon. Finding none, he stood and pressed the button for the hotel lobby, and the elevator restarted its descent.

The camera mounted high up in one corner of the elevator ceiling began to eat away at Markio's nerves, so he handed Lil' Mark's gun to Star and she put it in her Chanel bag. Mya picked up Lil' Mark's iPhone, scowled at her older brother, and ended the FaceTime call.

When the elevator doors parted, Mya gave Markio a one-armed hug, then pulled the Mac-10 from inside her purse and held Pee Wee at gunpoint.

"Star, call the police," Mya said. "Markio and Reggie, y'all need to get the fuck outta here. I'll tell the police Lil' Mark tried to rob us, and I'm pretty sure this camera will back me up on that."

Markio took one last look at Lil' Mark just as his old childhood friend coughed out another crimson mist. Lil' Mark was taking deep, gasping breaths, one hand clawing weakly at his bullet-riddled abdomen. The blood had continued to spread, soaking through his entire shirt. His face seemed to have gotten paler in the last twenty seconds.

Reggie grabbed the sleeve of Markio's shirt and pulled, and the two of them walked hurriedly out of the elevator and across the hotel lobby, ignoring the frightened stares of the two front desk clerks who had obviously heard the gunshots. One of them was already on the phone with police.

Markio's ears were still ringing as he stepped out into the fresh night air. He had parked his Benz truck close to the door, and Reggie's candy blue 1987 Chevy Caprice on gold 28-inch Forgiato rims was parked a few spaces over. They separated without a word and jumped into their vehicles, and Markio followed the flashy blue Caprice to the parking lot's exit.

Reggie made the right turn that would take him back into the heart of Michigan City.

But Markio was undecided.

He could turn left and get on Interstate 94, which would take him to Chicago, where his younger cousin Bankroll Reese could very easily assist him in squashing the beef with Worm and Bam. Bam was the highest ranking TVL in their neighborhood, but Reese had more money, which meant Reese ultimately had more power. And besides, there were dozens of other gang members from the hood who would undoubtedly take Markio's side over Worm's.

Or Markio could make the right turn and follow behind Reggie, heading back into town and preparing himself for whatever the police and Leezo and Worm had in store for him here in Michigan City, Indiana.

He didn't have to think long about it; the five million dollars he had stashed in the bedroom at his mother's house made the decision for him.

He hit the right-hand turn signal and stepped down on the gas pedal.

To Be Continued...
Super Gremlin 2
Coming Soon

Lock Down Publications and Ca$h Presents assisted publishing packages.

BASIC PACKAGE $499
Editing
Cover Design
Formatting

UPGRADED PACKAGE $800
Typing
Editing
Cover Design
Formatting

ADVANCE PACKAGE $1,200
Typing
Editing
Cover Design
Formatting
Copyright registration
Proofreading
Upload book to Amazon

LDP SUPREME PACKAGE $1,500
Typing
Editing
Cover Design
Formatting
Copyright registration
Proofreading
Set up Amazon account

Upload book to Amazon
Advertise on LDP Amazon and Facebook page

***Other services available upon request. Additional
charges may apply
Lock Down Publications
P.O. Box 944
Stockbridge, GA 30281-9998
Phone # 470 303-9761

Submission Guideline

Submit the first three chapters of your completed manuscript to ldpsubmissions@gmail.com, subject line: Your book's title. The manuscript must be in a .doc file and sent as an attachment. Document should be in Times New Roman, double spaced and in size 12 font. Also, provide your synopsis and full contact information. If sending multiple submissions, they must each be in a separate email.

Have a story but no way to send it electronically? You can still submit to LDP/Ca$h Presents. Send in the first three chapters, written or typed, of your completed manuscript to:

LDP: Submissions Dept
Po Box 944
Stockbridge, Ga 30281

DO NOT send original manuscript. Must be a duplicate.

Provide your synopsis and a cover letter containing your full contact information.

Thanks for considering LDP and Ca$h Presents.

<u>NEW RELEASES</u>

THE MURDER QUEENS 3 by MICHAEL GALLON

GORILLAZ IN THE TRENCHES 3 by SAYNOMORE

SALUTE MY SAVAGERY by FUMIYA PAYNE

SUPER GREMLIN by KING RIO

Super Gremlin

Coming Soon from Lock Down Publications/Ca$h Presents

BLOOD OF A BOSS **VI**

SHADOWS OF THE GAME II

TRAP BASTARD II

By **Askari**

LOYAL TO THE GAME **IV**

By **T.J. & Jelissa**

TRUE SAVAGE **VIII**

MIDNIGHT CARTEL IV

DOPE BOY MAGIC IV

CITY OF KINGZ III

NIGHTMARE ON SILENT AVE II

THE PLUG OF LIL MEXICO II

CLASSIC CITY II

By **Chris Green**

BLAST FOR ME **III**

A SAVAGE DOPEBOY III

CUTTHROAT MAFIA III

DUFFLE BAG CARTEL VII

HEARTLESS GOON VI

By **Ghost**

A HUSTLER'S DECEIT III

KILL ZONE II

BAE BELONGS TO ME III

TIL DEATH II

By **Aryanna**

KING OF THE TRAP III

King Rio

By **T.J. Edwards**
GORILLAZ IN THE BAY V
3X KRAZY III
STRAIGHT BEAST MODE III
De'Kari
KINGPIN KILLAZ IV
STREET KINGS III
PAID IN BLOOD III
CARTEL KILLAZ IV
DOPE GODS III
Hood Rich
SINS OF A HUSTLA II
ASAD
YAYO V
Bred In The Game 2
S. Allen
THE STREETS WILL TALK II
By Yolanda Moore
SON OF A DOPE FIEND III
HEAVEN GOT A GHETTO III
SKI MASK MONEY III
By Renta
LOYALTY AIN'T PROMISED III
By Keith Williams
I'M NOTHING WITHOUT HIS LOVE II
SINS OF A THUG II
TO THE THUG I LOVED BEFORE II

Super Gremlin

IN A HUSTLER I TRUST II

By Monet Dragun

QUIET MONEY IV

EXTENDED CLIP III

THUG LIFE IV

By **Trai'Quan**

THE STREETS MADE ME IV

By **Larry D. Wright**

IF YOU CROSS ME ONCE III

ANGEL V

By **Anthony Fields**

THE STREETS WILL NEVER CLOSE IV

By K'ajji

HARD AND RUTHLESS III

KILLA KOUNTY IV

By Khufu

MONEY GAME III

By Smoove Dolla

JACK BOYS VS DOPE BOYS IV

A GANGSTA'S QUR'AN V

COKE GIRLZ II

COKE BOYS II

LIFE OF A SAVAGE V

CHI'RAQ GANGSTAS V

SOSA GANG III

BRONX SAVAGES II

BODYMORE KINGPINS II

BLOOD OF A GOON II

By Romell Tukes

MURDA WAS THE CASE III

Elijah R. Freeman

AN UNFORESEEN LOVE IV

BABY, I'M WINTERTIME COLD III

By **Meesha**

QUEEN OF THE ZOO III

By **Black Migo**

CONFESSIONS OF A JACKBOY III

By Nicholas Lock

KING KILLA II

By Vincent "Vitto" Holloway

BETRAYAL OF A THUG III

By Fre$h

THE BIRTH OF A GANGSTER III

By Delmont Player

TREAL LOVE II

By Le'Monica Jackson

FOR THE LOVE OF BLOOD III

By Jamel Mitchell

RAN OFF ON DA PLUG II

By Paper Boi Rari

HOOD CONSIGLIERE III

By Keese

PRETTY GIRLS DO NASTY THINGS II

Super Gremlin

By Nicole Goosby
LOVE IN THE TRENCHES II
By Corey Robinson
IT'S JUST ME AND YOU II
By Ah'Million
FOREVER GANGSTA III
By Adrian Dulan
THE COCAINE PRINCESS IX
SUPER GREMLIN II
By King Rio
CRIME BOSS II
Playa Ray
LOYALTY IS EVERYTHING III
Molotti
HERE TODAY GONE TOMORROW II
By Fly Rock
REAL G'S MOVE IN SILENCE II
By Von Diesel
GRIMEY WAYS IV
By Ray Vinci
SALUTE MY SAVAGERY II
By Fumiya Payne

King Rio

Super Gremlin

KING OF NEW YORK I II,III IV V

RISE TO POWER I II III

COKE KINGS I II III IV V

BORN HEARTLESS I II III IV

KING OF THE TRAP I II

By **T.J. Edwards**

IF LOVING HIM IS WRONG…I & II

LOVE ME EVEN WHEN IT HURTS I II III

By **Jelissa**

WHEN THE STREETS CLAP BACK I & II III

THE HEART OF A SAVAGE I II III IV

MONEY MAFIA I II

LOYAL TO THE SOIL I II III

By **Jibril Williams**

A DISTINGUISHED THUG STOLE MY HEART I II & III

LOVE SHOULDN'T HURT I II III IV

RENEGADE BOYS I II III IV

PAID IN KARMA I II III

SAVAGE STORMS I II III

AN UNFORESEEN LOVE I II III

BABY, I'M WINTERTIME COLD I II

By **Meesha**

A GANGSTER'S CODE I &, II III

A GANGSTER'S SYN I II III

THE SAVAGE LIFE I II III

CHAINED TO THE STREETS I II III

BLOOD ON THE MONEY I II III

King Rio

A GANGSTA'S PAIN I II III
By J-Blunt
PUSH IT TO THE LIMIT
By **Bre' Hayes**
BLOOD OF A BOSS **I, II, III, IV, V**
SHADOWS OF THE GAME
TRAP BASTARD
By **Askari**
THE STREETS BLEED MURDER **I, II & III**
THE HEART OF A GANGSTA I II& III
By **Jerry Jackson**
CUM FOR ME I II III IV V VI VII VIII
An **LDP Erotica Collaboration**
BRIDE OF A HUSTLA **I II & II**
THE FETTI GIRLS **I, II& III**
CORRUPTED BY A GANGSTA I, II III, IV
BLINDED BY HIS LOVE
THE PRICE YOU PAY FOR LOVE I, II ,III
DOPE GIRL MAGIC I II III
By **Destiny Skai**
WHEN A GOOD GIRL GOES BAD
By **Adrienne**
THE COST OF LOYALTY I II III
By Kweli
A GANGSTER'S REVENGE **I II III & IV**
THE BOSS MAN'S DAUGHTERS I II III IV V
A SAVAGE LOVE **I & II**

174

Super Gremlin

BAE BELONGS TO ME I II
A HUSTLER'S DECEIT I, II, III
WHAT BAD BITCHES DO I, II, III
SOUL OF A MONSTER I II III
KILL ZONE
A DOPE BOY'S QUEEN I II III
TIL DEATH
By **Aryanna**
A KINGPIN'S AMBITON
A KINGPIN'S AMBITION **II**
I MURDER FOR THE DOUGH
By **Ambitious**
TRUE SAVAGE I II III IV V VI VII
DOPE BOY MAGIC I, II, III
MIDNIGHT CARTEL I II III
CITY OF KINGZ I II
NIGHTMARE ON SILENT AVE
THE PLUG OF LIL MEXICO II
CLASSIC CITY
By **Chris Green**
A DOPEBOY'S PRAYER
By **Eddie "Wolf" Lee**
THE KING CARTEL **I, II & III**
By **Frank Gresham**
THESE NIGGAS AIN'T LOYAL **I, II & III**
By **Nikki Tee**
GANGSTA SHYT **I II &III**

King Rio

By **CATO**

THE ULTIMATE BETRAYAL

By **Phoenix**

BOSS'N UP **I , II & III**

By **Royal Nicole**

I LOVE YOU TO DEATH

By **Destiny J**

I RIDE FOR MY HITTA

I STILL RIDE FOR MY HITTA

By **Misty Holt**

LOVE & CHASIN' PAPER

By **Qay Crockett**

TO DIE IN VAIN

SINS OF A HUSTLA

By **ASAD**

BROOKLYN HUSTLAZ

By **Boogsy Morina**

BROOKLYN ON LOCK I & II

By **Sonovia**

GANGSTA CITY

By **Teddy Duke**

A DRUG KING AND HIS DIAMOND I & II III

A DOPEMAN'S RICHES

HER MAN, MINE'S TOO I, II

CASH MONEY HO'S

THE WIFEY I USED TO BE I II

PRETTY GIRLS DO NASTY THINGS

176

Super Gremlin

By Nicole Goosby

TRAPHOUSE KING **I II & III**

KINGPIN KILLAZ I II III

STREET KINGS I II

PAID IN BLOOD **I II**

CARTEL KILLAZ I II III

DOPE GODS I II

By **Hood Rich**

LIPSTICK KILLAH **I, II, III**

CRIME OF PASSION I II & III

FRIEND OR FOE I II III

By **Mimi**

STEADY MOBBN' **I, II, III**

THE STREETS STAINED MY SOUL I II III

By **Marcellus Allen**

WHO SHOT YA **I, II, III**

SON OF A DOPE FIEND I II

HEAVEN GOT A GHETTO I II

SKI MASK MONEY I II

Renta

GORILLAZ IN THE BAY **I II III IV**

TEARS OF A GANGSTA I II

3X KRAZY I II

STRAIGHT BEAST MODE I II

DE'KARI

TRIGGADALE I II III

MURDAROBER WAS THE CASE I II

King Rio

Elijah R. Freeman
GOD BLESS THE TRAPPERS I, II, III
THESE SCANDALOUS STREETS I, II, III
FEAR MY GANGSTA I, II, III IV, V
THESE STREETS DON'T LOVE NOBODY I, II
BURY ME A G I, II, III, IV, V
A GANGSTA'S EMPIRE I, II, III, IV
THE DOPEMAN'S BODYGAURD I II
THE REALEST KILLAZ I II III
THE LAST OF THE OGS I II III
Tranay Adams
THE STREETS ARE CALLING
Duquie Wilson
MARRIED TO A BOSS I II III
By Destiny Skai & Chris Green
KINGZ OF THE GAME I II III IV V VI VII
CRIME BOSS
Playa Ray
SLAUGHTER GANG I II III
RUTHLESS HEART I II III
By Willie Slaughter
FUK SHYT
By Blakk Diamond
DON'T F#CK WITH MY HEART I II
By Linnea
ADDICTED TO THE DRAMA I II III
IN THE ARM OF HIS BOSS II

Super Gremlin

By Jamila
YAYO I II III IV
A SHOOTER'S AMBITION I II
BRED IN THE GAME
By S. Allen
TRAP GOD I II III
RICH $AVAGE I II III
MONEY IN THE GRAVE I II III
By Martell Troublesome Bolden
FOREVER GANGSTA I II
GLOCKS ON SATIN SHEETS I II
By Adrian Dulan
TOE TAGZ I II III IV
LEVELS TO THIS SHYT I II
IT'S JUST ME AND YOU
By Ah'Million
KINGPIN DREAMS I II III
RAN OFF ON DA PLUG
By Paper Boi Rari
CONFESSIONS OF A GANGSTA I II III IV
CONFESSIONS OF A JACKBOY I II
By Nicholas Lock
I'M NOTHING WITHOUT HIS LOVE
SINS OF A THUG
TO THE THUG I LOVED BEFORE
A GANGSTA SAVED XMAS
IN A HUSTLER I TRUST

King Rio

By Monet Dragun
CAUGHT UP IN THE LIFE I II III
THE STREETS NEVER LET GO I II III
By Robert Baptiste
NEW TO THE GAME I II III
MONEY, MURDER & MEMORIES I II III
By **Malik D. Rice**
LIFE OF A SAVAGE I II III IV
A GANGSTA'S QUR'AN I II III IV
MURDA SEASON I II III
GANGLAND CARTEL I II III
CHI'RAQ GANGSTAS I II III IV
KILLERS ON ELM STREET I II III
JACK BOYZ N DA BRONX I II III
A DOPEBOY'S DREAM I II III
JACK BOYS VS DOPE BOYS I II III
COKE GIRLZ
COKE BOYS
SOSA GANG I II
BRONX SAVAGES
BODYMORE KINGPINS
BLOOD OF A GOON
By Romell Tukes
LOYALTY AIN'T PROMISED I II
By Keith Williams
QUIET MONEY I II III
THUG LIFE I II III

Super Gremlin

EXTENDED CLIP I II

A GANGSTA'S PARADISE

By **Trai'Quan**

THE STREETS MADE ME I II III

By **Larry D. Wright**

THE ULTIMATE SACRIFICE I, II, III, IV, V, VI

KHADIFI

IF YOU CROSS ME ONCE I II

ANGEL I II III IV

IN THE BLINK OF AN EYE

By **Anthony Fields**

THE LIFE OF A HOOD STAR

By **Ca$h & Rashia Wilson**

THE STREETS WILL NEVER CLOSE I II III

By **K'ajji**

CREAM I II III

THE STREETS WILL TALK

By **Yolanda Moore**

NIGHTMARES OF A HUSTLA I II III

By **King Dream**

CONCRETE KILLA I II III

VICIOUS LOYALTY I II III

By **Kingpen**

HARD AND RUTHLESS I II

MOB TOWN 251

THE BILLIONAIRE BENTLEYS I II III

REAL G'S MOVE IN SILENCE

King Rio

By Von Diesel

GHOST MOB

Stilloan Robinson

MOB TIES I II III IV V VI

SOUL OF A HUSTLER, HEART OF A KILLER I II

GORILLAZ IN THE TRENCHES I II III

By SayNoMore

BODYMORE MURDERLAND I II III

THE BIRTH OF A GANGSTER I II

By Delmont Player

FOR THE LOVE OF A BOSS

By C. D. Blue

MOBBED UP I II III IV

THE BRICK MAN I II III IV V

THE COCAINE PRINCESS I II III IV V VI VII VIII

SUPER GREMLIN

By King Rio

KILLA KOUNTY I II III IV

By Khufu

MONEY GAME I II

By Smoove Dolla

A GANGSTA'S KARMA I II III

By FLAME

KING OF THE TRENCHES I II III

by **GHOST & TRANAY ADAMS**

QUEEN OF THE ZOO I II

By **Black Migo**

Super Gremlin

GRIMEY WAYS I II III

By Ray Vinci

XMAS WITH AN ATL SHOOTER

By Ca$h & Destiny Skai

KING KILLA

By Vincent "Vitto" Holloway

BETRAYAL OF A THUG I II

By Fre$h

THE MURDER QUEENS I II III

By Michael Gallon

TREAL LOVE

By Le'Monica Jackson

FOR THE LOVE OF BLOOD I II

By Jamel Mitchell

HOOD CONSIGLIERE I II

By Keese

PROTÉGÉ OF A LEGEND I II III

LOVE IN THE TRENCHES

By Corey Robinson

BORN IN THE GRAVE I II III

By Self Made Tay

MOAN IN MY MOUTH

By XTASY

TORN BETWEEN A GANGSTER AND A GENTLEMAN

By J-BLUNT & Miss Kim

LOYALTY IS EVERYTHING I II

Molotti

King Rio

HERE TODAY GONE TOMORROW

By Fly Rock

PILLOW PRINCESS

By S. Hawkins

NAÏVE TO THE STREETS

WOMEN LIE MEN LIE I II III

GIRLS FALL LIKE DOMINOS

STACK BEFORE YOU SPURLGE

FIFTY SHADES OF SNOW I II III

By A. Roy Milligan

SALUTE MY SAVAGERY

By Fumiya Payne

<u>BOOKS BY LDP'S CEO, CA$H</u>

TRUST IN NO MAN

TRUST IN NO MAN 2

TRUST IN NO MAN 3

BONDED BY BLOOD

SHORTY GOT A THUG

THUGS CRY

THUGS CRY 2

THUGS CRY 3

TRUST NO BITCH

TRUST NO BITCH 2

TRUST NO BITCH 3

TIL MY CASKET DROPS

RESTRAINING ORDER

RESTRAINING ORDER 2

IN LOVE WITH A CONVICT

LIFE OF A HOOD STAR

XMAS WITH AN ATL SHOOTER

King Rio

9 781960 993083